NGŨGĨ WA THIONG'O was born in Limuru, Kenya, in 1938. He was educated at the Alliance High School, Kikuyu, at Makerere University, Uganda and at the University of Leeds.

His first novel, *Weep Not, Child*, was published in 1964 and this was followed by *The River Between* (1965), *A Grain of Wheat* (1967), and *Petals of Blood* (1977). *Devil on the Cross* (1980), was conceived and written during the author's one-year detention in prison, in Kenya, where he was held without trial after the performance by peasants and workers of his play *Ngaahika Ndeenda (I Will Marry When I Want)*. This was his first novel to be published in his own language, Gĩkũyũ, and then translated into English and many other languages. *Matigari* was published in Gĩkũyũ in Kenya in 1986 and this is the only English translation. The author has also written collections of short stories, plays and numerous essays.

Ngũgĩ is an active campaigner for the African language and form, and he writes, travels and lectures extensively on this theme. His work is known throughout the world and has made a powerful impact both at home and overseas.

Wangũi wa Goro is a social critic, interpreter, writer and translator, with strong interest in the development of African languages. She writes and recites poetry, and will be publishing a work of non-fiction on *Mekatilili* in 1989 (Vita Books). She has translated all of Ngũgĩ's children's books into English (Heinemann Kenya Ltd).

NGŨGĨ WA THIONG'O

WEEP NOT, CHILD

HEINEMANN

Heinemann International
a division of Heinemann Educational Books Ltd
Halley Court, Jordan Hill, Oxford OX2 8EJ

Heinemann Educational Books Inc
361 Hanover Street, Portsmouth, New Hampshire, 03801, USA

Heinemann Educational Books (Nigeria) Ltd
PMB 5205, Ibadan
Heinemann Kenya Ltd
PO Box 45314, Nairobi, Kenya
Heinemann Educational Boleswa
PO Box 10103, Village Post Office, Gaborone, Botswana
Heinemann Publishers (Caribbean) Ltd
175 Mountain View Avenue, Kingston 6, Jamaica

LONDON   EDINBURGH   MELBOURNE   SYDNEY
AUCKLAND   SINGAPORE   MADRID
HARARE   ATHENS   BOLOGNA

First published in the African Writers Series in 1964
First published in this edition, 1987

British Library Cataloguing in Publication Data

Ngũgĩ Thiong'o
Weep not, child.—
(African writers series)
I. Title   II. Series
823[F]   PR9381.9.N45

ISBN 0-435-90830-8
ISBN 0-435-90831-6 Export pbk.

Printed in Great Britain by
Cox & Wyman Ltd, Reading, Berkshire

90 91 92 93 94 10 9 8 7 6 5 4 3

Weep not, child
Weep not, my darling
With these kisses let me remove your tears,
The ravening clouds shall not be long victorious,
They shall not long possess the sky . . .

WALT WHITMAN
On the Beach at Night

for JASBIR KALSI

PART ONE

THE WANING LIGHT

CHAPTER ONE

Nyokabi called him. She was a small, black woman, with a bold but grave face. One could tell by her small eyes full of life and warmth that she had once been beautiful. But time and bad conditions do not favour beauty. All the same, Nyokabi had retained her full smile – a smile that lit up her dark face.

'Would you like to go to school?'

'O, mother!' Njoroge gasped. He half feared that the woman might withdraw her words. There was a little silence till she said,

'We are poor. You know that.'

'Yes, mother.' His heart pounded against his ribs slightly. His voice was shaky.

'So you won't be getting a mid-day meal like other children.'

'I understand.'

'You won't bring shame to me by one day refusing to attend school?'

O mother, I'll never bring shame to you. Just let me get there, just let me. The vision of his childhood again opened before him. For a time he contemplated the vision. He lived in it alone. It was just there, for himself; a bright future . . . Aloud he said, 'I like school.'

He said this quietly. His mother understood him.

'All right. You'll begin on Monday. As soon as your father gets his pay we'll go to the shops. I'll buy you a shirt and a pair of shorts.'

O, mother, you are an angel of God, you are, you are. Then he wondered. Had she been to a magic worker? Or else how could she have divined his child's unspoken wish, his undivulged dream? *And here I am, with nothing but a piece of*

3

calico on my body and soon I shall have a shirt and shorts for the first time.

'I thank you mother, very much.' He wanted to say more. But Njoroge was not used to expressing strong feelings in words. However his eyes spoke all. Again Nyokabi understood. She was happy.

When Kamau came in the evening, Njoroge took him aside.

'Kamau, I shall go to school.'

'School?'

'Yes.'

'Who said so? Father?'

'No. It was our mother. Has our elder mother told you the same thing?'

'No, brother. You know I am being trained as a carpenter. I cannot drop the apprenticeship. But I am glad you're going to school.'

'I am, oh, so glad. But I wish you too would come.'

'Don't you worry about me. Everything will be all right. Get education, I'll get carpentry. Then we shall, in the future, be able to have a new and better home for the whole family.'

'Yes,' Njorogo said thoughfully. 'That's what I want. And you know, I think Jacobo is as rich as Mr Howlands because he got education. And that's why each takes his children to school because of course they have learnt the value of it.'

'It's true. But some, you know, must get learning and others this and that trade.'

'Well, you see, I was thinking that if both of us could learn and become like John, the big son of Jacobo, it would be a good thing. People say that because he has finished all the learning in Kenya, he will now go far away to ...'

'England.'

'Or Burma.'

'England and Burma and Bombay and India are all the same places. You have to cross the sea before you can reach there.'

'That's where Mr Howlands comes from?'

4

'Yes.'

'I wonder why he left England, the home of learning, and came here. He must be foolish.'

'I don't know. You cannot understand a white man.'

There was only one road that ran right across the land. It was long and broad and shone with black tar, and when you travelled along it on hot days you saw little lakes ahead of you. But when you went near, the lakes vanished, to appear again a little farther ahead. Some people called them the devil's waters because they deceived you and made you more thirsty if your throat was already dry. And the road which ran across the land and was long and broad had no beginning and no end. At least, few people knew of its origin. Only if you followed it it would take you to the big city and leave you there while it went beyond to the unknown, perhaps joining the sea. Who made the road? Rumour had it that it came with the white men and some said that it was rebuilt by the Italian prisoners during the Big War that was fought far away from here. People did not know how big the war had been because most of them had never seen a big war fought with planes, poison, fire and bombs – bombs that would finish a country just like that when they were dropped from the air. It was indeed a big war because it made the British worry and pray and those black sons of the land who had gone to fight said it was a big war. There was once another big war. The first one was to drive away the Germans who had threatened to attack and reduce the black people to slavery. Or so the people had been told. But that was far away and long ago and only old men and middle-aged men could remember it. It was not as big as the second because then there were no bombs, and black people did not go to Egypt and Burma.

The Italian prisoners who built the long tarmac road had left a name for themselves because some went about with black women and the black women had white children. Only the children by black mothers and Italian prisoners who were also

5

white men were not really 'white' in the usual way. They were ugly and some grew up to have small wounds all over the body and especially around the mouth so that flies followed them all the time and at all places. Some people said that this was a punishment. Black people should not sleep with white men who ruled them and treated them badly.

Why should the white men have fought? Aaa! You could never tell what these people would do. In spite of the fact that they were all white, they killed one another with poison, fire and big bombs that destroyed the land. They had even called the people to help them in killing one another. It was puzzling. You could not really understand because although they said they fought Hitler (ah! Hitler, that brave man, whom all the British feared, and he was never killed you know, just vanished like that), Hitler too was a white man. That did not take you very far. It was better to give up the attempt and be content with knowing the land you lived in, and the people who lived near you. And if this was not enough and you wanted to see more people and hear stories from far and wide – even stories from across the sea, Russia, England, Burma – you could avoid the vigilance of your wife and go to the local town, Kipanga. You could, for instance, tell her that you were going to buy some meat for the family. That was something.

'All right! Go and don't loiter in the town too much. I know you men. When you want to avoid work you go to the town and drink while we, your slaves, must live in toil and sweat.'

'I'll come back soon.'

'See how you turn your eyes. You cannot even look at me in the face because you know you'll go and stay there the whole day. . . .'

'Now, now, just you trust me to come back soon.'

'The idea of trusting you!'

There were many ways from Mahua village to Kipanga. You could follow the big road. It passed near the town. Or you could follow a track that went through a valley into the town.

In a country of ridges, such as Kikuyuland, there are many valleys and small plains. Even the big road went through a valley on the opposite side. Where the two met they had as it were embraced and widened themselves into a plain. The plain, more or less rectangular in shape, had four valleys leading into or out of it at the corners. The first two valleys went into the Country of the Black People. The other two divided the land of the Black People from the land of the White People. This meant that there were four ridges that stood and watched one another. Two of the ridges on the opposite sides of the long sides of the plain were broad and near one another. The other two were narrow and had pointed ends. You could tell the land of Black People because it was red, rough and sickly, while the land of the white settlers was green and was not lacerated into small strips.

Kipanga town was built in this field. It was not a big town like the big city. However, there was one shoe factory and many black people earned their living there. The Indian shops were many. The Indian traders were said to be very rich. They too employed some black boys whom they treated as nothing. You could never like the Indians because their customs were strange and funny in a bad way. But their shops were big and well-stocked with things. White settlers, with their wives and children, often came to the rich Indians and bought all they wanted. The Indians feared Europeans and if you went to buy in a shop and a white man found you, the Indian would stop selling to you and, trembling all over, would begin to serve him. But some said that this was a cunning way to deceive the white women because when the Indian trembled and was all 'Yes, please, Memsahib, anything more?' the women would be ready to pay any price they were told because they thought an Indian who feared them dared not cheat about prices.

Black people too bought things from the Indians. But they also bought in the African shops which stood alone on one side of the town near the post office. The Africans had not many things in their store and they generally charged higher

7

prices so that although the Indians were not liked and they abused women, using dirty words they had learnt in Swahili, people found it wiser and more convenient to buy from them. Some people said that black people should stick together and take trade only to their black brethren. And one day an old poor woman said, 'Let Africans stick together and charge very low prices. We are all black. If this be not so, then why grudge a poor woman the chance to buy from someone, be he white or red, who charges less money for his things?'

In the Indian bazaar, black people mingled with white people and Indians. You did not know what to call the Indian. Was he also a white man? Did he too come from England? Some people who had been to Burma said that Indians were poor in their country and were too ruled by white men. There was a man in India called Gandhi. This man was a strange prophet. He always fought for the Indian freedom. He was a thin man and was always dressed poorly in calico stretched over his bony body. Walking along the shops, you could see his photograph in every Indian building. The Indians called him *Babu*, and it was said the Babu was actually their god. He had told them not to go to war so that while black people had been conscripted into the army the Indians had utterly refused and had been left alone. It was rumoured that the white men in Kenya did not like them because they had refused to go to war against Hitler. This showed that the Indians were cowards. The Africans were inclined to agree with this idea of Indian cowardice.

The African shops were built in two rows which faced one another. The air was full of noise and, near the meat shops, there was a strong stench of burning flesh. Some young men spent all their time doing nothing but loitering in the shops. Some could work the whole day for a pound of meat. They were called the lazy boys and people in the village said that such men would later turn to stealing and crime. This thought always made people shudder because murder in cold-blood was a foul thing. A man who murdered was for ever a curse in heaven and earth. One could recognize such boys because they

8

were to be seen hanging around teashops, meat shops and even in the Indian bazaar, waiting for any errand that might earn them a day's meal. At times they called themselves young Hitlers.

The barber's shop was a famous place. The barber himself was a short brown man with hair very carefully brushed. He was very funny and he could tell stories which made people laugh. The barber knew everybody and everybody knew him. He was not called by any other name except the barber. If you said that you did not know who the barber was, or where his shop was, people at once knew that you were either a stranger or a fool. A fool, in the town's vocabulary, meant a man who had a wife who would not let him leave her lap even for a second. How could anyone afford not to call on the barber who knew how to sing and dance and could speak English?

'I learnt it during the Big War.'

'And it was all that big?'

(The barber lets his clippers go flick – lick – lick – lick. Everyone stands expectantly by waiting to hear about the Big War. The barber takes his time.)

'My man, you would not ask that if you had been there. What with bombs and machine guns that went boom-crunch! boom-crunch! troo! troo! and grenades and people crying and dying! Aha, I wish you had been there.'

'Maybe it was like the first war?'

'Ha! ha! ha! That was a baby's war. It was only fought here. Those Africans who went to that one were only porters. But this one . . . (Turn your head this way. No, this way. Yes, that's it.) this one, we carried guns and we shot white men.'

'White men?'

'Y-e-e-e-s. They are not the gods we had thought them to be. We even slept with their women.'

'Ha! How are they—?'

'Not different. Not different. I like a good fleshy black body with sweat. But they are . . . you know . . . so thin . . . without flesh . . . nothing.'

'But it was wonderful to. . . .'

'Well! Before you started . . . you thought . . . it was eh – eh – wonderful. But after . . . it was nothing. And you had to pay some money.'

'Are there—?'

'Many! Many who were willing to sell. And that was in Jerusalem of all places.'

People around became amazed.

'You don't mean to say that there's such a place as Jerusalem?'

'Ha, ha, ha! You don't know. You don't know. We have seen things and places. There now, you're ready. No! wait a minute (flick-lick). That's all right now. You look smart. Had you been to Jerusalem—'

'It is getting late!'

'I must go. I must buy something for those at home.'

'Me too. Told my women that I would come and buy meat for them. Now it's almost dark.'

'These women!'

'O yes, women!'

And with these words, Ngotho made his way through the crowd into the open. He always loved to listen to the barber. Somehow the talk reminded him of his own travels and troubles in the First World War. As a boy he had been conscripted and made to carry things for the fighting white men. He also had to clear dark bush and make roads. Then, he and the others were not allowed to use guns. But in the barber's war! Ah! that was something. His own two sons had also gone to this one. Only one had returned. And the one who had returned never talked much about the actual war, except to say that it had been a terrible waste of life.

Ngotho bought four pounds of meat. But they were bound into two bundles each of two pounds. One bundle was for his first wife, Njeri, and the other for Nyokabi, his second wife. A husband had to be wise in these affairs otherwise a small flaw or apparent bias could easily generate a civil war in the family. Not that Ngotho feared this very much. He knew that his two wives liked each other and were good companions and friends. But you could not quite trust women. They were fickle and very jealous. When a woman was angry no amount of beating would pacify her. Ngotho did not beat his wives much. On the contrary, his home was well known for being a place of peace. All the same, one had to be careful.

He went across the fields. He did not want to follow the big road or the valley because these two were long. He wondered what Nyokabi and Njeri would say. He had not kept his word to be back soon. But then, he had not intended to come home soon. His wives were good women. It was not easy to get such women these days. It was quite true what the barber had said about a fleshy, black body with sweat. Look at that Memsahib in whose husband's employment he was. She was so thin that Ngotho at times wondered if the woman had flesh at all. What did a man want such a wife for? A man wanted a fat woman. Such a woman he had in Njeri and Nyokabi especially when he married them. But time had changed them . . . He wondered if the barber had quite told the truth – that bit about going with a white woman. Who could believe that a white woman like Mrs Howlands could make herself cheap enough to go with black men for money? Yet one could believe anything these days. He wondered if his son Boro had done such a thing. Of course, it was something to have a son who had – but the thought of buying was not at all nice. And if they had nothing extra, well, it was better to have a black woman.

'How quick you've been!' Nyokabi welcomed him.

'You know men are always v-e-r-y quick,' added Njeri in the same sarcastic tone. The two women usually stayed together to 'hasten' or 'shorten' the night. Ngotho was inwardly pleased. He knew that when they adopted that tone they meant to be friendly.

'I went to the barber.'

11

'As if we could not have used a razor-blade to clear off your hair.'

'Well, times are changing. As Bwana Howlands says—'

'You want to be a modern white man.'

'You are two troublesome women. Take this meat first.'

Nyokabi took her share, and Njeri hers.

'Now it's time for me to go and disturb the young people,' said Njeri. All the sons of Ngotho with other young men and women from Mahua ridge were in Njeri's hut. They usually went there to shorten the night. At such times Njeri would leave the young people and she would go to sit with Nyokabi. When they went to Nyokabi's hut she too would do likewise, leave them, and go to visit Njeri. But some nights, the young people wanted to hear stories from Ngotho or from the women. At such times they all would be in the same place.

'Tell Njoroge to come and show his new clothes to his father,' Nyokabi told Njeri as the latter left.

Ngotho was proud that his son would start learning. When anybody now asked him whether he had taken any of his sons to school, he would proudly say, '*Yes!*' It made him feel almost equal to Jacobo.

'When is he beginning?'

'On Monday.'

'Does he like the idea?'

'He looked happy.'

She was right. Njoroge's heart had felt like bursting with happiness and gratitude when he had known that he, like Mwihaki, the daughter of Jacobo, would start learning how to read and write.

CHAPTER TWO

On Monday, Njoroge went to school. He did not quite know where it was. He had never gone there, though he knew the direction to it. Mwihaki took him and showed him the way. Mwihaki was a young girl. Njoroge had always admired her. Once some herd-boys had quarrelled with Mwihaki's brothers. They had thrown stones and one had struck her. Then the boys had run away followed by her brothers. She had been left alone crying. Njoroge who had been watching the scene from a distance now approached and felt like soothing the weeping child. Now she, the more experienced, was taking him to school.

Mwihaki was a daughter of Jacobo. Jacobo owned the land on which Ngotho lived. Ngotho was a *Muhoi*. Njoroge had never come to understand how his father had become a *Muhoi*. Maybe a child did not know such matters. They were too deep for him. Jacobo had small boys and one big son and big daughter. The big daughter was a teacher. Her name was Lucia. Njoroge always thought Lucia a nice name. All his sisters had ugly names. Not like Lucia.

The other boys were rough. They laughed at him and made coarse jokes that shocked him. His former high regard of schoolboys was shaken. He thought that he would never like to make such jokes. Nyokabi, his mother, would be angry if he did.

One boy told him, 'You are a *Njuka*.'

'No! I am not a *Nju-u-ka*,' he said.

'What are you?'

'I am Njoroge.'

They laughed heartily. He felt annoyed. Had he said anything funny?

Another boy commanded him, 'Carry this bag. You're a *Njuka*.'

13

He was going to take it. But Mwihaki came to his rescue.

'He is my *Njuka*. You cannot touch him.' Some laughed. Others sneered.

'Leave Mwihaki's *Njuka* alone.'

'He is Mwihaki's boy.'

'He'll make a good husband. A *Njuka* to be a husband of Mwihaki.'

'A *Njuka* is a *Njuka*. He must carry my bag for me.'

All this talk embarrassed and confused Njoroge. He did not know what to do. Mwihaki was annoyed. She burst out, 'Yes, he is my *Njuka*. Let any of you touch him.'

Silence followed. Njoroge was grateful. Apparently the boys feared her because her sister was a teacher and Mwihaki might report them.

The school looked a strange place. But fascinating. The church, huge and hollow, attracted him. It looked haunted. He knew it was the House of God. But some boys shouted while they were in there. This too shocked him. He had been brought up to respect all holy places, like graveyards and the bush around fig trees.

The teacher wore a white blouse and a green skirt. Njoroge liked the white and green because it was like a blooming white flower on a green plant. Grass in this country was green in wet weather and flowers bloomed white all over the land, especially in Njahi season. Njoroge, however, feared her when two days later she beat a boy, whack! whack! ('Bring the other hand') whack! whack! whack! The stick broke into bits. Njoroge could almost feel the pain. It was as if it was being communicated to him without physical contact. The teacher looked ugly while she punished. Njoroge hated seeing anybody being thrashed and he was sorry for the boy. But he should not have bullied a *Njuka*. It was on that day that Njoroge learnt that *Njuka* was the name given to a new-comer.

Njoroge usually kept alone. And he always reached home earlier than the other boys of the village. He did not want to reach home in the dark. Bad boys walked slowly after school for if they reached home early they would be asked to help in the evening chores. When they reached home they said, 'Teacher Lucia (or Isaac) kept us late.'

But sometimes they were found out and they were beaten. Njoroge did not like being beaten.

After three weeks he made his mother angry. It was the fault of Mwihaki. She had asked him to wait for her so they might go home together. After all, their homes were near each other. Besides, she said she feared certain boys. Njoroge was pleased. Together they took the road home slowly, chatting. When they reached the top of the hill that was near their village, they sat there and began playing. It was sweet to play with a girl and especially if that girl came from a family higher up the social scale than one's own. She looked more precious because rare. She was small and delicate. He soon forgot that the sun was sinking while he and Mwihaki competed in throwing stones to see who could throw the farthest. And that was the time his mother had come and seen them. Nyokabi had watched the sun slowly sink home without her son appearing. She had become worried about him and with an anxious heart had come to look for him. Njoroge was not beaten. But he knew too well that she was annoyed. She did not want her son to associate with a family of the rich because it would not be healthy for him.

Njoroge thought it all Mwihaki's fault. And he thought her a bad girl and promised himself that he would not play with her any more. Or even wait for her.

He came home one day and found his mother shelling some castor-oil seeds from their pods. She often did this and when she accumulated enough after a number of months she sold them at the market.

'Mother, let me help you.'

'Go and do your school work first.'

Nyokabi was proud of having a son in school. It made her soul happy and light-hearted whenever she saw him bending double over a slate or recounting to her what he had seen at school. She felt elated when she ordered her son to go and do some reading or some sums. It was to her the greatest reward she would get from her motherhood if she one day found her son writing letters, doing arithmetic and speaking English. She tried to imagine what the Howlands woman must have felt to have a daughter and a son in school. She wanted to be the same. Or be like Juliana. Juliana was the wife of Jacobo and she must surely have felt proud to have a daughter who was a teacher and a son who would probably be flying to foreign parts soon. That was something. That was real life. It did not matter if anyone died poor provided he or she could one day say. 'Look, I've a son as good and as well-educated as any you can find in the land.'

You did not need to be educated to know this. Her mother's instinct that yearned for something broader than that which could be had from her social circumstances and conditions saw this. That was why she had impressed on her husband Ngotho the need for one son to be learned. Her other son had died in the Big War. It had hurt her much. Why should he have died in a white man's war? She did not want to sacrifice what was hers to other people. If Njoroge could now get all the white man's learning, would Ngotho even work for Howlands and especially as the wife was reputed to be a hard woman? Again, would they as a family continue living as *Ahoi* in another man's land, a man who clearly resented their stay. A lot of motives had indeed combined into one desire, the desire to have a son who had acquired all the learning that there was. These days she even thought that if she had much money she would send her married daughters to school. All would then have a schooling that would at least enable them to speak English.

'Mother, you must tell me all those stories again,' he implored as he knelt down to help in spite of her rejection of his offer.

'Hmmmm,' she murmured as she blew some rubbish away

16

from the seeds she had in her hands. She paused for a moment and smiled.

'You cunning young man. Is that why you offered to help, eh?'

'Mother, you must,' he said earnestly.

'Why *must* I?' she asked carelessly as she resumed her work.

'I was told to tell a story today. The story you told us about the *Irimu* came to mind. But when I stood in front of the class and all eyes were fixed on me, I was afraid.' He paused. 'I lost the story.' He finished dramatically in a tragic tone as if such incidents rarely happened.

'A man should never be afraid. You should have scratched your head for another story. You have many. Or do your elder mother and myself waste our time telling you all those stories about the tribe?'

'I tell you, mother, I forgot all of them.' He pleaded with such great vigour that Nyokabi was forced to laugh. Njoroge could be very serious about certain things. But now he too laughed. He loved his mother so when she laughed. She had rich milk-white teeth which time had done nothing to harm.

'*Ni wega*, all right. I'll tell you some in the evening. . . . Oh, I forgot. Your mother wants you to run for your brother. Now do that at once.'

He went into the hut, threw down his slate, and then rushed out.

'Njoroge! Njoroge!'

He came back.

'Don't you take off your school clothes?'

He felt ashamed. He should not have forgotten. He went back to the hut and took off the school clothes. He put on the old piece of calico. This too had been part of the contract. It was necessary to preserve the clothes intact for as long as possible.

The path he followed passed just below Mwihaki's home. The houses were hidden by a big hedge of growing fir trees that surrounded the household. You could see the corrugated iron roof and the wooden walls of the imposing building through an opening or two in the hedge. Njoroge had been there, out in the courtyard, a number of times when he and others went to collect money for picking pyrethrum flowers for Jacobo. The place looked like a European's house and Njoroge was always over-awed by the atmosphere around the whole compound. He had never been in the big building and he was always curious to know what the inside looked like.

But he had once been in the kitchen. The kitchen was a separate building, a round, mud-walled, grass-thatched hut that was used for all the cooling. It was also where the servants slept. He had been to that kitchen on Christmas Day when many children who usually worked for Jacobo were invited for a party by Juliana. She was a fat woman, with a beautiful round face and haughty eyes. But she was kind with children and on that occasion she had bought much bread. How appetizing it all looked as it lay on a tray nearby, forming a sharp-pointed gleaming white hill! Njoroge's mouth had watered and he had a lot of difficulty in swallowing the saliva for fear of making some audible sound at the throat which would betray him to his hostess and her children. But the tragic part of the day's proceedings came when they were all told to shut their eyes for Grace. It was during the Grace that one child had made a funny sound which had at once made Njoroge giggle. But no sooner did he begin giggling than he was joined by another, who giggled even more loudly, till both of them now burst out in open laughter which in turn caused the long Grace to be cut short. The children were hungry. Juliana was annoyed and gave Njoroge and all the children there assembled a long lecture. If they (the unfortunate two) had been her own children who had misbehaved, she said quite clearly that they would have gone without a meal for two days. But her children would never have done such a thing. She had brought them up to value *Ustaarabu,* and the rules of good manners. She had concluded her speech by saying that it was her considered

18

opinion that all children should be brought up as she did hers. Because people, however, did not do this, she never liked her children to associate with primitive homes. Njoroge sensed that the way he had been brought up was being criticized. It was on that day that Njoroge had come to value Mwihaki for after the lecture she had taken greater interest in him, perhaps to soothe his hurt feelings. All this was a long way back.

Before Njoroge went very far, he saw her coming along the same path but from the opposite direction. If he went on he would meet her. Suddenly he realized that he did not want to meet her while he had on that piece of calico which, when blown by the wind, left the lower part of his body without covering. For a time, he was irresolute and hated himself for feeling as he did about the clothes he had on. Before he had started school, in fact even while he made that covenant with his mother, he would never have thought that he would ever be ashamed of the calico, the only dress he had ever known since birth.

He turned to the left and followed another path. All around him was the sloping pyrethrum field that belonged to Jacobo. Below, a forest. Further down still were the Indian and African shops. But only a few roofs could be seen. The land belonging to Mr Howlands was adjacent to one of the smaller, narrow ridges which could be seen on the right. That was where Ngotho, Njoroge's father, worked. Njoroge always passed near there on his way to school.

He left the pyrethrum field, took another turn to join the route he had avoided and then went into the next field. He could just see Nganga's household. Nganga was the village carpenter. Kamau was apprenticed to him. Ngotho had to pay a huge fattened he-goat and a hundred and fifty shillings on top. Nganga was rich. He had land. Any man who had land was considered rich. If a man had plenty of money, many motor cars, but no land, he could never be counted as rich. A man who went with tattered clothes but had at least an acre of red earth was better off than the man with money. Nganga could afford three wives, although he was younger than Ngotho. He had not been to the first or indeed the second war. But he was said to be clever, although he was a little bit rough and not quite honest. Everybody in the village took a panga, a jembe or a knife to him for the repair of their handles. He also repaired broken fences and made tables and beds of all sorts. And he could tell a story. This was considered a good thing for a man.

Njoroge had not reached the court-yard when he saw his brother coming. Kamau had just finished his duties. Njoroge was glad when he saw him for, although Kamau was older, they got on well.

'Let's go brother,' said Kamau as he pulled Njoroge by the hand. He looked gloomy.

'Today, you're late.'

'It is *this* man!'

Njoroge thought that something was wrong. It was not often that his brother was so angry.

'Is he not a good man?'

'Good man! If I didn't know that father would be annoyed after paying all that money, I would stop coming here. I have now been with him for six months yet it was only yesterday that he first allowed me to handle a plane. He is always telling me, "Hold here! Hold there", and always asking me to watch and note carefully. How can a man learn by watching without practice? Surely not by sweeping the yard and taking away the rubbish and carrying the tools for him. But if I touch something! And you know,' and here Kamau spoke in disgust, 'his youngest wife actually makes me hold her child just as if she was a European woman and I her Ayah. Oh dear me! It is such a dirty little thing that keeps on howling and—!'

'Why don't you tell father?'

'You don't know. Father would obviously take Nganga's side, especially on the question of watching, because this is how people used to learn trades in the olden times. They don't realize that things are changing!'

They kept silent for a while as they made their way home in the gathering gloom, the prelude to darkness. Then Njoroge, as if he had suddenly thought up a great question, asked, 'But why does he treat you like that? He is a black man?'

'Blackness is not all that makes a man,' Kamau said bitterly. 'There are some people, be they black or white, who don't want others to rise above them. They want to be the source of all knowledge and share it piecemeal to others less endowed. That is what's wrong with all these carpenters and men who have a certain knowledge. It is the same with rich people. A rich man does not want others to get rich because he wants to be the only man with wealth.'

'Probably,' Njoroge said, impressed. He had never heard Kamau speak so much at length.

'. . . Some Europeans are better than Africans.'

Again Njoroge was impressed.

'That's why you at times hear father say that he would rather work for a white man. A white man is a white man. But a black man trying to be a white man is bad and harsh.'

Njoroge could not quite follow Kamau. But he pitied his brother and vowed that he himself would not become a carpenter. The only good thing was education. He tried to change the subject.

'Mother will tell us a story.'

'Oh, will she?'

Both loved stories. Story-telling was a common entertainment in their family. Kori, like Ngotho, was a good story-teller and could keep a whole company listening and laughing. Boro, who had been to the war, did not know many tribal stories. He drank a lot and he was always sad and withdrawn. He never talked much about his war experiences except when he was drunk or when he was in a mood of resentment against the Government and settlers.

'We fought for them, we fought to save them from the hands of their white brothers. . . .'

Then on such occasions, he might talk just a little about

the actual fighting. But he very rarely alluded to Mwangi's death. It was common knowledge that they had loved each other very much. Before the war, it had always been said that such love between brothers was unnatural and portended no good.

Boro, Kori and Kamau were all sons of Njeri, Ngotho's eldest wife. Njoroge's only true brother was Mwangi who had died in the war. But they all behaved as if they were of one mother. Kori worked in an African tea-shop called Green Hotel. Green Hotel was a very dirty place, full of buzzing flies, while the stench of decay hung in the air like a heavy cloud. But it was a very popular place because there was a wireless set. Njoroge looked forward to Kori's homecoming because he brought with him the town gossip and what was happening in the country. For instance, when Jomo came from Britain, it was Kori who brought the news home. Home was especially a nice place when all the brothers and many village girls and boys came in the evening and, sitting around the fireplace in a big circle, they would gossip, laugh and play. Njoroge always longed for the day he would be a man, for then he would have the freedom to sit with big circumcised girls and touch them as he saw the young men do. But sometimes his brothers did not come. Home then was dull. But the mothers could tell stories. And Ngotho too, when he was in the mood.

'Our elder mother wanted you,' Njoroge said when they reached home. It was already dark. While Njeri was always 'our' or 'my elder mother', Nyokabi, being the younger wife, was always just 'mother'. It was a habit observed and accepted by all.

'What does she want?'

'I don't know.'

Kamau began to move. Njoroge stood and watched in silence. Then he raised his voice, 'Remember to come back to our hut. You remember the story.'

'Yes,' Kamau replied. His voice sounded thin in the dark.

Later in the evening Kamau came to Nyokabi's hut.

22

'Tell us the story.'

'Now, now, don't be troublesome,' Nyokabi said.

'It is a bad woman this. If I had been my father, I would not have married her.' Kamau liked teasing Nyokabi. Tonight his teasing sounded forced. It did not provoke laughter.

'Oh! But he could not resist me.'

'It isn't true,' said Ngotho who just then entered the hut. 'You should have seen how happy she was when I proposed to her. Nobody could have taken her. So I pitied her.'

'I refused all the young men that wanted me. But your father would have died if I had refused him.'

'Don't you believe a word she says!'

Ngotho was given food. He began to eat and for a time there was an awkward silence. The children could not joke in their father's presence. Njoroge broke the silence.

'Tell us a story. You promised, you know.'

'You children! You never ask your father to tell you stories. Tonight he *will* tell you,' she said smilingly towards her husband. She was happy.

'If you all come to my *Thingira*, I'll tell you one or two.'

Njoroge feared his father. But it always made him feel good to listen to him.

'... There was wind and rain. And there was also thunder and terrible lightning. The earth and the forest around Kerinyaga shook. The animals of the forest whom the Creator had recently put there were afraid. There was no sunlight. This went on for many days so that the whole land was in darkness. Because the animals could not move, they just sat and moaned with wind. The plants and trees remained dumb. It was, our elders tell us, all dead except for the thunder, a violence that seemed to strangle life. It was this dark night whose depth you could not measure, not you or I can conceive of its solid blackness, which would not let the sun pierce through it.

'But in this darkness, at the foot of Kerinyaga, a tree rose. At first it was a small tree and grew up, finding a way even through

23

the darkness. It wanted to reach the light, and the sun. This tree had *Life*. It went up, up, sending forth the rich warmth of a blossoming tree – you know a holy tree in the dark night of thunder and moaning. This was Mukuyu, God's tree. Now, you know that at the beginning of things there was only one man (Gikuyu) and one woman (Mumbi). It was under this Mukuyu that he first put them. And immediately the sun rose, and the dark night melted away. The sun shone with a warmth that gave life and activity to all things. The wind and lightning and thunder stopped. The animals stopped wondering and moved. They no longer moaned but gave homage to the Creator and Gikuyu and Mumbi. And the Creator who is also called Murungu took Gikuyu and Mumbi from his holy mountain. He took them to the country of ridges near Siriana and there stood them on a big ridge before he finally took them to Mukuruwe wa Gathanga about which you have heard so much. But he had shown them all the land – yes, children, God showed Gikuyu and Mumbi all the land and told them,

"This land I hand over to you. O Man and woman
It's yours to rule and till in serenity sacrificing
Only to me, your God, under my sacred tree . . ." '

There was something strange in Ngotho's eyes. He looked as if he had forgotten all about those who were present, Kamau, Njoroge, Boro, Kori and many other young men and women who had come to make the long hours of night shorter by listening to stories. It was as if he was telling a secret for the first time, but to himself. Boro sat in a corner. The expression on his face could not be seen. He did not once move but kept on looking past his father. It was as if Boro and Ngotho were the only two who were there at the beginning when these things came to be. Njoroge too could imagine the scene. He saw the sun rise and shine on a dark night. He saw fear, gloom and terror of the living things of the creator, melting away, touched by the warmth of the holy tree. It must have been a new world. The man and woman must have been blessed to walk in the

24

new Kingdom with Murungu. He wished he had been there to stand near Him in His holy place and survey all the land. Njoroge could not help exclaiming,

'Where did the land go?'

Everyone looked at him.

'. . . I am old now. But I too have asked that question in waking and sleeping. I've said, "What happened, O Murungu, to the land which you gave to us? Where, O Creator, went our promised land?" At times I've wanted to cry or harm my body to drive away the curse that removed us from the ancestral lands. I ask, "Have you left your children naked, O Murungu?"

'I'll tell you. There was a big drought sent to the land by evil ones who must have been jealous of the prosperity of the children of the Great One. But maybe also the children of Mumbi forgot to burn a sacrifice to Murungu. So he did not shed His blessed tears that make crops grow. The sun burnt freely. Plague came to the land. Cattle died and people shrank in size. Then came the white man as had long been prophesied by Mugo wa Kibiro, that Gikuyu seer of old. He came from the country of ridges, far away from here. Mugo had told the people of the coming of the white man. He had warned the tribe. So the white man came and took the land. But at first not the whole of it.

'Then came the war. It was the first big war. I was then young, a mere boy, although circumcised. All of us were taken by force. We made roads and cleared the forest to make it possible for the warring white man to move more quickly. The war ended. We were all tired. We came home worn out but very ready for whatever the British might give us as a reward. But, more than this, we wanted to go back to the soil and court it to yield, to create, not to destroy. But Ng'o! The land was gone. My father and many others had been moved from our ancestral lands. He died lonely, a poor man waiting for the white man to go. Mugo had said this would come to be. The white

25

man did not go and he died a *Muhoi* on this very land. It then belonged to Chahira before he sold it to Jacobo. I grew up here, but working . . . (here Ngotho looked all around the silent faces and then continued) . . . working on the land that belonged to our ancestors. . . .'

'You mean the land that Howlands farms?' Boro's voice was cracked, but clear.

'Yes. The same land. My father showed it all to me. I have worked there too, waiting for the prophecy to be fulfilled.'

'And do you think it will ever be fulfilled?' It was Kori who asked this to break the silence that followed Ngotho's reply.

'I don't know. Once in the country of the ridges where the hills and ridges lie together like lions, a man rose. People thought that he was the man who had been sent to drive away the white man. But he was killed by wicked people because he said people should stand together. I've waited for the prophecy. It may not be fulfilled in my life time . . . but O, Murungu, I wish it could.'

Someone coughed. Then silence. From a corner, a young man tried to make a joke about the coming of the white man and what people thought of his skin. Nobody heeded him. He laughed alone and then stopped. For Njoroge, it was a surprising revelation, this knowledge that the land occupied by Mr Howlands originally belonged to them.

Boro thought of his father who had fought in the war only to be dispossessed. He too had gone to war, against Hitler. He had gone to Egypt, Jerusalem and Burma. He had seen things. He had often escaped death narrowly. But the thing he could not forget was the death of his step-brother, Mwangi. For whom or for what had *he* died?

When the war came to an end, Boro had come home, no longer a boy but a man with experience and ideas, only to find that for him there was to be no employment. There was no land on which he could settle, even if he had been able to do so. As he listened to this story, all these things came into his mind with a growing anger. How could these people have let the white man occupy the land without acting? And what was all this superstitious belief in a prophecy?

In a whisper that sounded like a shout, he said, 'To hell with the prophecy.'

Yes, this was nothing more than a whisper. To his father, he said, 'How can you continue working for a man who has taken your land? How can you go on serving him?'

He walked out, without waiting for an answer.

CHAPTER THREE

Ngotho left early for work. He did not go through the fields as was his usual custom. Ngotho loved the rainy seasons when everything was green and the crops in flower, and the morning dew hung on the leaves. But the track where he had disturbed the plants and made the water run off made him feel as if, through his own fault, he had lost something. There was one time when he had felt a desire to touch the dew-drops or open one and see what it held hidden inside. He had trembled like a child but, after he had touched the drops and they had quickly lost shape melting into wetness, he felt ashamed and moved on. At times he was thankful to Murungu for no apparent reason as he went through these cultivated fields all alone while the whole country had a stillness. Almost like the stillness of death.

This morning he walked along the road – the big tarmac road that was long and broad and had no beginning and no end except that it went into the city. Motor cars passed him. Men and women, going to work, some in the settled area and some in the shoe factory, chattered along. But Ngotho was not aware of anything that went by him. Why had he behaved like that in front of all those children? The voice of Boro had cut deep into him, cut into all the lonely years of waiting. Perhaps he and others had waited for too long and now he feared that this was being taken as an excuse for inactivity, or, worse, a betrayal.

He came to the Indian shops. Years ago, he had worked here. That was long before the Second War. He had worked for an Indian who had always owed him a month's pay. This was deliberate. It was meant to be a compelling device to keep Ngotho in the Indian's employment permanently. For if he left, he would lose a month's pay. In the end, he had to lose it. That was the time he went to work for Mr Howlands – as a Shamba-boy. But at first he did everything from working in the tea plantations to cleaning the big house and carrying firewood. He passed through the African shops, near the barber's shop, and went on, on to the same place where he had now been for years, even before the second Big War took his two sons away to kill one and change the other.

Mr Howlands was up. He never slept much. Not like Mem-sahib who sometimes remained in bed until ten o'clock. She had not much else to do. There was something in Howlands, almost a flicker of mystery, that Ngotho could never fathom.

'Good morning, Ngotho.'

'Good morning, Bwana.'

'Had a good night?'

'Ndio Bwana.'

Ngotho was the only man Mr Howlands greeted in this fashion – a fashion that never varied. He spoke in the usual abstract manner as if his mind was preoccupied with something big. It was at any rate something that took all his attention. His mind was always directed towards the *shamba*. His life and soul were in the *shamba*. Everything else with him counted only in so far as it was related to the *shamba*. Even his wife mattered only in so far as she made it possible for him to work in it more efficiently without a worry about home. For he left the management of home to her and knew nothing about what happened there. If he employed someone in the house, it was only because his wife had asked for an extra 'boy'. And if she later beat the 'boy' and wanted him sacked, well, what did it matter? It was not just that the boys had black skins. The question of wanting to know more about his servants just never crossed his mind.

The only man he had resisted the efforts of his wife to have sacked was Ngotho. Not that Mr Howlands stopped to analyse his feelings towards him. He just loved to see Ngotho working in the farm; the way the old man touched the soil, almost fond-ling, and the way he tended the young tea plants as if they were his own. .... Ngotho was too much of a part of the farm to be separated from it. Something else. He could manage the farm-labourers as no other person could. Ngotho had come to him at a time when his money position was bad. But with the coming of Ngotho, things and his fortune improved. Mr Howlands was tall, heavily built, with an oval-shaped face that ended in a double chin and a big stomach. In physical appearance at least, he was a typical Kenya settler. He was a product of the First World War. After years of security at home, he had been sud-denly called to arms and he had gone to the war with the fire of youth that imagines war a glory. But after four years of blood and terrible destruction, like many other young men he was utterly disillusioned by the 'peace'. He had to escape. East Africa was a good place. Here was a big trace of wild country to conquer.

For a long time England remained a country far away. He did not want to go back because of what he remembered. But he soon found that he wanted a wife. He could not go about with the natives as some had done. He went back 'home', a stranger, and picked the first woman he could get. Suzannah was a good girl – neither beautiful nor ugly. She too was bored with life in England. But she had never known what she wanted to do. Africa sounded quite a nice place so she had willingly followed this man who would give her a change. But she had not known that Africa meant hardship and complete break with Europe. She again became bored. Mr Howlands was ob-livious of her boredom. He believed her when she had told him, out in England, that she could face the life in the bush.

But she soon had a woman's consolation. She had her first child, a son. She turned her attention to the child and the ser-vants at home. She could now afford to stay there all the day long playing with the child and talking to him. She found sweet pleasure in scolding and beating her servants. The boy, Peter, was followed by a girl. For a time, the three – mother, daughter and son – made home, the father only appearing in the evening. It was lucky that their home was near Nairobi. The children could go to school there. Her pride was in watching them grow together loving each other. They in their way loved her. But Peter soon took to his father. Mr Howlands grew to like his son and the two walked through the fields together. Not that Mr Howlands was demonstrative. But the thought that he would have someone to whom he could leave the *shamba* gave him a glow in his heart. Each day he became more and more of a family man and, as years went by, seemed even reconciled to that England from which he had run away. He sent both children back for studies. Then European civilization caught up with him again. His son had to go to war.

Mr Howlands lost all faith – even the few shreds that had begun to return. He would again have destroyed himself, but again his god, land, came to the rescue. He turned all his efforts and energy into it. He seemed to worship the soil. At times he went on for days with nothing but a few cups of tea. His one pleasure was in contemplating and planning the land to which he had now given all his life. Suzannah was left alone. She beat and sacked servant after servant. But God was kind to her. She had another boy, Stephen. He was now an only son. The daughter had turned missionary after Peter's death in the war.

They went from place to place, a white man and a black man. Now and then they would stop here and there, examine a luxuriant green tea plant, or pull out a weed. Both men admired this *shamba*. For Ngotho felt responsible for whatever happened to this land. He owed it to the dead, the living and the unborn of his line, to keep guard over this *shamba*. Mr Howlands always felt a certain amount of victory whenever he walked through it all. He alone was responsible for taming this unoccupied wildness. They came to a raised piece of ground and stopped. The land sloped gently to rise again into the next ridge and the next. Beyond Ngotho could see the African Reserve.

'You like all this?' Mr Howlands asked absent-mindedly. He was absorbed in admiring the land before him.

'It is the best land in all the country,' Ngotho said emphatically. He meant it. Mr Howlands sighed. He was wondering if Stephen would ever manage it after him.

'I don't know who will manage it after me. . . .'

Ngotho's heart jumped. He too was thinking of his children. Would the prophecy be fulfilled soon?

'*Kwa nini Bwana.* Are you going back to—?'

'No,' Mr Howlands said, unnecessarily loudly.

'. . . Your home, home. . . .'

'My home is here!'

Ngotho was puzzled. Would these people never go? But had not the old Gikuyu seer said that they would eventually return the way they had come? And Mr Howlands was thinking, Would Stephen really *do*? He was not like the other one. He felt the hurt and the pain of loss.

'The war took him away.'

Ngotho had never known where the other son had gone to. Now he understood. He wanted to tell of his own son: he longed to say, 'You took him away from me'. But he kept quiet. Only he thought Mr Howlands should not complain. It had been his war.

CHAPTER FOUR

At school Njoroge proved good at reading. He always remembered his first lesson. The teacher had stood in front. He was a short man with a small moustache which he was fond of touching and fondling. They called him Isaka. This was his Christian name, a corruption of Isaac. The children rarely knew a teacher's surname. Many stories went around about Isaka. Some said that he was not *a good Christian*. This meant that he drank and smoked and went about with women, a thing which no teacher in their school was expected to do. But Isaka was a jovial man and children loved him. Njoroge admired his moustache. It was claimed that Isaka folded his moustache mischievously whenever he was talking with the women teachers. It was a source of constant gossip to the boys whenever they were alone in groups. When the teacher had come in he made a strange mark on the board.

'A'. This was meaningless to Njoroge and others.

Teacher Say Ah.
Class Aaaaa.
Teacher Again.
Class Aaaaa.

One felt the corrugated iron roof would crack.

Teacher (making another mark on the board) Say Eee.
Class Eeeeeeee.

That sounded nice and familiar. When a child cried he said, Eeeee, Eeeee.

Teacher I.
Class Iiiiiii.
Teacher Again.
Class Iiiiiii.
Teacher That's the old Gikuyu way of saying 'Hodi', 'may I come in?'

The children laughed. It was so funny the way he said this. He made yet another mark on the board. Njoroge's heart beat fast. To know that he was actually learning! He would have a lot to tell his mother.

Teacher Oh.
Class Ooooo.
Teacher Again.
Class Ooooo.

Another letter:

Teacher U.
Class Uuu.
Teacher What does a woman say when she sees danger?
Class (the boys looking triumphantly at the girls) Uuuuuuu.

There was laughter.

Teacher Say U-u-u-u-u.
Class U-u-u-u-u-u-u-u.
Teacher What animal says this?

A boy shot up his arm. But before he could answer, the class had burst out 'a dog'. Again there was laughter and a little confused murmuring.

Teacher What does a dog do?

Here there was disagreement. Some shouted that it said, U-u-u-u-u, while others simply declared that a dog barked.

Teacher A dog barks.
Class A dog barks.
Teacher What does a dog say when it barks?
Class U-u-u-u-u-u.

From that day the teacher's name had become U-u.

Njoroge loved these reading practices, especially the part of blabbering and laughing and shouting as one liked. At first when he reached home, he had tried to teach Kamau. But Kamau resented this, and Njoroge had to give up the idea.

Mwihaki said to him, 'Why do you keep alone – to avoid me?'

Njoroge felt ashamed. He still remembered that day his mother met them both playing on the hill. She had not rebuked him. But a mother's silence is the worst form of punishment for it is left to one's imagination to conjure up what is in her mind. Njoroge, however, wanted to appear respectable and dignified in the eyes of Mwihaki.

'You always come out late,' he at last said, rather timidly. They went on together. School was just over for the day. As they walked, they saw birds flying across the fields. She broke the silence.

'No, I don't come out late. It's you. You try to avoid me.'

'Do your parents beat you?' she asked after another silence.

'No. Not often, only when I do wrong.'

Mwihaki wondered how this boy could do wrong. Njoroge appeared so docile, withdrawn, and always went home in time.

'Why do you ask?' Njoroge continued.

'Well, I was thinking that if they don't beat you, that would explain why you are not afraid of them.'

'Do yours beat you?' he asked sympathetically. She looked soft, small and delicate. Perhaps all girls were naughty.

'Yes – sometimes. And when mother does not beat me, she uses bad language which hurts me more than beating. I fear her.'

'I too fear my parents.' He did not want to criticize them in front of her. He always remembered an Indian boy who once gave him a sweet, wanting to be friendly. Njoroge had then been with his mother. He was surprised by this act of kindness from an Indian boy because he had never thought that an Indian was capable of such. He took the sweet. He was going to put it into his mouth when his mother turned on him and shouted, 'Is it that you have not eaten anything for a whole year? Are you to be greedily taking anything you're given by anyone, even by a dirty little Indian?'

Njoroge threw it away. But it had hurt him because the boy saw him do this. He both ached and feared to go back and tell him something. But he did not then go. Days later he went to the same place. The boy was not there.

'Do you think parents are always right?'

'I think so. I don't know. But you sometimes feel you know something inside here. . . . Don't you feel that way sometimes?'

'I do!' he said, not wishing to appear ignorant.

They soon forgot their parents and laughed. Sometimes they played. Njoroge was rather reserved. But Mwihaki was more playful. She picked flowers and threw them at him. He liked this and wanted to retaliate but he did not like plucking a flower in bloom because it lost colour. He said, 'Let's not play with flowers.'

'Oh, but I love flowers.'

They passed near Mr Howland's house. It was huge and imposing. It was more grand than that which belonged to Mwihaki's father.

'My father works here.'

'This place belongs to Mr Howlands.'

36

'You know him?'

'No. But my father talks about him. My father visits him and says that he is the best farmer in all the land.'

'Are they friends?'

'I don't know. I don't think so. Europeans cannot be friends with black people. They are so high.'

'Have you been here to his farm?'

'No!'

'I have often come here to see father. There is a boy about my height. His skin is so very white. I think he is the son of Mr Howlands. I did not like the way he clung to his mother's skirt, a frightened thing. Yet his eyes were fixed on me. A bit curious. The second time he was alone. When he saw me, he rose and walked in my direction. I was frightened because I did not know what he wanted. I ran. He stood still and watched me. Then he walked back. Whenever I go there I make sure I am near my father.'

'Did he want to speak to you?'

'Well, I don't know. He may have wanted to quarrel with me. He is like his father. And you know—'

Njoroge remembered the story Ngotho had told them. He could not tell Mwihaki of this. This was to be his own secret.

'All this land belongs to black people.'

'Y-e-e-s. I've heard father say so. He says that if people had had education, the white man would not have taken all the land. I wonder why our old folk, the dead old folk, had no learning when the white man came?'

'There was nobody to teach them English.'

'Y-e-s. That could be it,' she said doubtfully.

'Is your class taught English?'

'Oh, no. It is only Standard IV which is taught English.'

'Does your father know how to speak English?'

'I think so.'

'Where did he learn it?'

'In the mission place . . . Siriana.'

'You'll learn English before me.'

'Why?'

'You're a class ahead of me.'

She considered this for a few minutes. Then she suddenly brightened up and said, 'I'll be teaching you....'

Njoroge did not like this. But he did not say so.

At the beginning of next year he was promoted to the third class. It was called Standard I for the other two were just pre-paratory – beginners' classes. The second beginners' class was found unnecessary for him. Standard I was the class that Mwihaki too would attend. Njoroge had caught up with her. He was glad. Before the school opened for the new year, Njoroge went to a forest with Kamau.

After a fruitless search for antelopes, he asked, 'Why don't you really start school?'

'You are always asking this.' Kamau laughed. But Njoroge remained serious. He always thought that schooling was the very best that a boy could have. It was the end of all living. And he wanted everyone to go to school.

'No!' Kamau continued, as he shook his head.

'Why?'

'Now, don't you pretend that you don't know the answer. Can't you see home? A man without land must learn to trade. Father has nothing. So what I am doing is important. If Nganga was not selfish, I would soon make a good carpenter. I could be rich and then we could all help you in school. Your learning is for all of us. Father says the same thing. He is anxious that you go on, so you might bring light to our home. Education is the light of Kenya. That's what Jomo says.'

Njoroge had heard of Jomo. When he came from across the sea, many people had gone to meet him in Nairobi. Njoroge thought that he would like to learn like Jomo and eventually cross the sea to the land of the white man. Mwihaki's brother was to go there soon.

In the evening, Ngotho glanced up at Njoroge.

'When will you open school?'

'On Monday.'

'Aaaaa,' Ngotho sighed. He now looked past his son. Nyokabi was preparing *Irio*. 'Education is everything,' Ngotho said. Yet he doubted this because he knew deep inside his heart that land was everything. Education was good only because it would lead to the recovery of the lost lands.

'You must learn to escape the conditions under which we live. It is a hard way. It is not much that a man can do without a piece of land.'

Ngotho rarely complained. He had all his life lived under the belief that something big would happen. That was why he did not want to be away from the land that belonged to his ancestors. That was really why he had faithfully worked for Mr Howlands, tending the soil carefully and everything that was in it. His son had come and with one stroke had made him doubt that very allegiance to Mr Howlands and the soil. And with this doubt had now come an old man's fear of his son. Boro had changed. This was all because of the war. Ngotho felt the war had dealt ill with him. It had killed one son! And the other was accusing him.

'The way Howlands looks at the farm!' he said slowly, to himself. Ngotho could not quite understand Mr Howlands' devotion to the soil. At times he looked so lost in it as if in escape from something else.

Njoroge listened to his father. He instinctively knew that an indefinable demand was being made on him, even though he was so young. He knew that for him education would be the fulfilment of a wider and more significant vision – a vision that embraced the demand made on him, not only by his father, but also by his mother, his brothers and even the village. He saw himself destined for something big, and this made his heart glow.

CHAPTER FIVE

A fairly large 'hill' stood outside Ngotho's household. Years of accumulating rubbish had brought this into being. If you stood there in the day time, you could more or less see the whole of the land of Jacobo. It was very big – as big as a settler's farm. The land was full of pyrethrum flowers and forests of black wattle trees. Jacobo was lucky because he had for many years been the only African allowed to grow pyrethrum. It was said that he had stood in the way of similar permits being given to other people. White farmers who planted it also did not want many Africans to be allowed to grow any cash crop like pyrethrum because this would lower the standards and quality of production.

Njoroge usually stood on this hill whenever he wanted to see his mother or brother coming from a distance. If he saw any of them he ran and helped them carry whatever they had. It did not matter if it was Njeri or any of her sons. The feeling of oneness was a thing that most distinguished Ngotho's household from many other polygamous families. Njeri and Nyokabi went to the *shamba* or market together. Sometimes they agreed amongst themselves that while one did that job the other would do this one. This was attributed to Ngotho, the centre of the home. For if you have a stable centre, then the family will hold.

It was a dark night. Njoroge and Kamau stood on the 'hill'. A few stars twinkled above. They looked like human eyes. Nyokabi had once told Njoroge that those were small holes through which one saw the lighted fire of God. He had not quite believed it.

'Do you see those distant lights?'

'Yes.'

'That's Nairobi, isn't it?' Njoroge's voice trembled slightly.

'Yes,' Kamau answered dreamily.

Njoroge peered through the darkness and looked beyond. Far away a multitude of lights could be seen. Above the host of lights was the grey haze of the sky. Njoroge let his eyes dwell on the scene. Nairobi, the big city, was a place of mystery that had at last called away his brothers from the family circle. The attraction of this strange city that was near and yet far weakened him. He sighed. He could not yet understand why his brothers had just decided to go. Like that.

'Do you think that they've found jobs?'

'Kori said that jobs there are plenty.'

'I see.'

'It is a big city. . . .'

'Yes – it – is – a – big – city.'

'Mr Howlands often goes there.'

'And Jacobo too. . . . Do you think they'll forget home?'

'I'm sure they won't. None can forget home.'

'Why couldn't they work here?'

'Do you think they didn't want to? You know this place. Even there where they go, they will learn that mere salary without a piece of land to cultivate is nothing. Look at Howlands. He is not employed by anybody. Yet he is very rich and happy. It's because he has land. Or look at Jacobo. He's like that because he has land. . . . Boro has no land. He could not get employment. You know how bitter he is with father because he says that it was through the stupidity of our fathers that the land had been taken. Do you think he could stay here? Boro is not of this place.'

Njoroge pondered this and wished he had been in a position to right the situation. Perhaps education. . . .

'Yes. Boro was strange.'

'He was often angry.'

'With father?'

'And all the old generation. And yet they tried.'

'To get the land?'

'Yes. Father said that people began pressing for their rights a long while back. Some went in a procession to Nairobi soon after the end of the first war to demand the release of their leader who had been arrested. People were shot and three of them died. You see people had thought that the young leader was the one who would make the white man go.'

'Father said this?'

'Yes. I found him telling Boro. You know father sort of fears Boro.'

'What did Boro say?'

'Nothing. He just sat there thinking or brooding over something. Boro is queer. Our elder mother says that it was the war that changed him. Some people say however that it is something to do with our other brother, the dead one.'

'Mwangi?'

'Yes. They say it is the British who killed him. But whether it was the British or not, it was a white man who did it.'

'Yes.'

They still peered through the darkness to the city that now held Boro and Kori. Kamau and Njoroge feared that the other two might be lost there. This would end the evening gathering of young men and women. But Kori had clearly said that they would be coming home from time to time.

'I too would like to leave this place!'

'Why?' Njoroge quickly asked. Njoroge's train of thought of what he would do for his family when he had money and learning was interrupted.

'Just a feeling. But first I must stop working for Nganga.'

'You have not finished the course.'

'I think I know enough carpentry to keep me going. I can now make a chair, a bed, and things like that.'

'And where will you go?'

'To the settled area. Or to Nairobi.'

Njoroge felt a strong desire to detain Kamau. He would miss him greatly.

'You may not get a job.'

'I will.'

'But have you forgotten about the strike?'

'Oh.'

'Yes. You know the intended strike that father is always talking about.'

'I don't know. I think strikes are for people like my father.'

'But father says that the strike is for all people who want the freedom of the black people.'

'Maybe. I cannot tell.'

They heard Njeri calling. They went down the 'hill'. As they went along, Njoroge remembered something he had wanted to ask about land.

'Do you think it's true what father says, that all the land belongs to black people?'

'Yes. Black people have their land in the country of black people. White men have their land in their own country. It is simple. I think it was God's plan.'

'Are there black people in England?'

'No. England is for white people only.'

'And they all left their country to come and rob us acres of what we have?'

'Yes. They are robbers.'

'All of them?'

'Yes. Even Mr Howlands.'

'Mr Howlands. . . . I don't like him. I did not like the way his son followed me once.'

'A lamb takes after its mother.'

Something occurred to him.

'Jacobo is a bad man. Do you think Mwi—' He stopped. Then he quickly changed the subject and asked, 'Who is Jomo?'

'Boro called him the Black Moses.'

'In the Bible?'

'I don't know.'

'I think I've heard about that in the Bible.'

Njeri's voice rang through the darkness. There was no more talk.

That night Njoroge stayed in bed for a little while before sleeping.

Njoroge did not want to be like his father working for a white man, or, worse, for an Indian. Father had said that the work was hard and had asked him to escape from the same conditions. Yes, he would. He would be different. And he would help all his brothers. Before he went to sleep he prayed, 'Lord, let me get learning. I want to help my father and mothers. And Kamau and all my other brothers. I ask you all this through Jesus Christ, our Lord, Amen.'

He remembered something else.

'... And help me God so that Mwihaki may not beat me in class. And God. . . .'

He fell asleep and dreamed of education in England.

Mwihaki was always pleased with Njoroge. She felt more secure with him than she felt with her brothers who did not care much about her. She confided in him and liked walking home with him. She was quite clever and held her own even among boys. And now that Njoroge was in her class she could ask him questions about class work. It was in Standard IV that they began to learn English.

Lucia, Mwihaki's sister, taught them. They all sat expectantly at their desk with eyes on the board. A knowledge of English was the criterion of a man's learning.

Stand = Rugama.
Teacher I am standing. What am I doing?
Class You are standing up.
Teacher Again.
Class You are standing up.
Teacher (pointing with a finger) You – no – you – yes. What's your name?
Pupil Njoroge.

Teacher Njoroge, stand up.

He stood up. Learning English was all right but not when he stood up for all eyes to watch and maybe make faces at him.

Teacher What are you doing?
Njoroge (thinly) You are standing up.
Teacher (slightly cross) What are *you* doing?
Njoroge (clears his throat, voice thinner still) You are standing up.
Teacher No, no! (to the class) Come on. What are *you, you* doing?

Njoroge was very confused. Hands were raised up all around him. He felt more and more foolish so that in the end he gave up the very attempt to answer.

Teacher (pointing to Mwihaki) Stand up. What are you doing?
Mwihaki (head bent on to one shoulder) I am standing up.
Teacher Good. Now, Njoroge. What is she doing?
Njoroge I am standing up.

The class giggled.

Teacher (very annoyed) Class, what is she doing?
Class (singing) You are standing up.
Teacher (still more angry) I am asking you. .... What is *she* doing?
Class (afraid, quietly singing) You are standing up.
Teacher Look here you stupid and lazy fools. How long do you take to catch things? Didn't we go over all this yesterday? If I come tomorrow and find that you make a single mistake I'll punish you all severely.

With this sharply-delivered threat, she walked out. Njoroge,

45

annoyed with himself at his poor showing, could now be heard trying to re-establish himself by telling them what they ought to have answered. 'She is standing up.' But one boy (the most stupid in the class) rebuked him. 'Why didn't you speak up when she was here, if you're so clever?'

After some more weeks of anger and threats the children managed to glean something of which they were very proud. Njoroge could now sing,

I am standing up.
You are standing up.
She is standing up.
We are standing up.
You are standing up.
They are standing up.
Where are you going?
I am going to the door.
We are going to the door.
Point to the blackboard. What are you doing?
I am pointing to the blackboard.

When a teacher came into the class, he greeted them in English.

Teacher Good morning children.
Class (standing up, singing the answer) Good morning Sir.

One day a European woman came to the school. As she was expected the school had been cleaned up and put in good order. The children had been told and shown how to behave. Njoroge had not seen many Europeans at very close quarters. He was now quite overawed by the whiteness and tenderness of this woman's skin. He wondered, What would I feel if I touched her skin? When she entered, the whole class stood up at attention. Some had already opened their mouths to answer the expected greeting.

'Good afternoon, children.'

'Good morning, Sir.'

Lucia felt like crying. Had she not taught them the correct thing over and over again? She had been let down. The visitor was explaining that since it was after lunch, after twelve o'clock, they should talk of 'afternoon', and since she was a woman they should call her 'Madam'.

'All right?'

'Yes Sir!'

'Madam!' shouted Lucia almost hysterically. She could have killed someone.

'Yes Madam.'

'Good afternoon.'

'Good afternoon, Madam.' But some still clung to 'Sir'. It had come to be part of their way of greeting. Even when one pupil greeted another 'Sir' accompanied the answer.

When the European went away, the children regretted the incident. Lucia beat them to cool her rage and shame. In future they were to know the difference between 'a morning' and 'an afternoon' and that between 'a Sir' and 'a Madam'.

'Yes, Madam.'

As they went home, Njoroge said to Mwihaki, 'You know, I had a feeling that I've seen that woman somewhere.'

'Have you? Where?'

'I don't know. It was just a feeling.'

They came to the place where Ngotho worked. She said, 'Do you still see the boy?'

'No! I think he has gone to school.'

'Did he ever try to speak to you again?'

'No! I've always avoided him. But he is always so alone.'

'Perhaps he has no brothers and sisters.'

'He can go and play with other children.'

'Where?'

They had gone only a few yards when Njoroge exclaimed, 'I know.'

'What?'

'Where I have seen that woman. I have seen her once o.

twice in Mr Howlands' place. I think it's their daughter. Father
says she is a mission woman.'

'Oh, yes. I've heard father say the same thing.'

'I wonder why she turned missionary. She is a settler's
daughter.'

'Perhaps she's different.'

'A lamb takes after its mother.' Kamau's proverb had just
come into his mind. He felt clever.

Kamau left Nganga and took a job with another carpenter at
the African shops. He did not go to Nairobi or the settled area
as he had intimated. Njoroge had won. But he saw that Kamau
was growing into a big *Kihii*, now ready for circumcision. Njoroge watched him with fear. When Kamau was initiated, he
would probably walk with men of his *Rika*. But this was not
just what he feared. After all, even now they were not very
much together. What he feared was that one day Kamau might
be drawn into the city. The other brothers had been called.
Though they came home quite regularly, yet they were changing. This was especially true of Kori. Kamau's going would
lead to a final family break-up and ruin the cosy security which
one felt in thinking of home. Kamau was the man of home. He
seemed to carry the family dumbly on his shoulders. Njoroge
sometimes went to the African shops to see him. The place was
always the same; men of all sorts hanging around the tea-shops
and slaughter houses, idling away the hours. The drudgery of
such a life made him fear a future that held in store such pur-
poseless living and weariness. He clung to books and whatever
the school had to offer. Njoroge was now fairly tall, black-
haired and brown-skinned, with clear large eyes. His features
were clear and well-defined – but perhaps too set for a boy of
his age.

Education for him, as for many boys of his generation, held
the key to the future. As he could not find companionship with
Jacobo's children (except Mwihaki), for these belonged to the
middle class that was rising and beginning to be conscious of

itself as such, he turned to reading. He read anything that came his way. The Bible was his favourite book. He liked the stories in the Old Testament. He loved and admired David, often identifying himself with this hero. The book of Job attracted him though it often gave rise to a painful stirring in his heart. In the New Testament, he liked the story of the young Jesus and the Sermon on the Mount.

Njoroge came to place faith in the Bible and with his vision of an educated life in the future was blended a belief in the righteousness of God. Equity and justice were there in the world. If you did well and remained faithful to your God, the Kingdom of Heaven would be yours. A good man would get a reward from God; a bad man would harvest bad fruits. The tribal stories told him by his mother had strengthened this belief in the virtue of toil and perseverance.

His belief in a future for his family and the village rested then not only on a hope for sound education but also on a belief in a God of love and mercy, who long ago walked on this earth with Gikuyu and Mumbi, or Adam and Eve. It did not make much difference that he had come to identify Gikuyu with Adam and Mumbi with Eve. To this God, all men and women were united by one strong bond of brotherhood. And with all this, there was growing up in his heart a feeling that the Gikuyu people, whose land had been taken by white men, were no other than the children of Israel about whom he read in the Bible. So although all men were brothers, the black people had a special mission to the world because they were the chosen people of God. This explained his brother's remark that Jomo was the Black Moses. Whenever he was with Mwihaki, he longed to impart some of these things to her. Yet when he tried to define them in words, he failed. So he kept them all to himself, walking alone in the fields and sometimes finding companionship with the nights.

CHAPTER SIX

Sometimes men came to see his father. Ever since Njoroge was a child, he had seen Ngotho as the centre of everything. As long as he lived, nothing could go wrong. And so Njoroge grew up, fearing his father, and yet putting implicit faith in him.

The men who came to see Ngotho usually went to his Thingira. But sometimes they went to Nyokabi's or Njeri's hut. This pleased Njoroge for he loved to listen to the mature talk of men. These men were the elders of the village. They talked about affairs of the land. Kori and Boro too brought men at week-ends, but these men were different from the young men of the village. The young men of the village usually allowed the elders to lead talks while they listened. But these others who came with Kori and Boro from the big city seemed to know a lot of things. They usually dominated the talks. And because most of them had been to the war, they were able to compare the affairs of the land with the lands to which they had been. They did not joke and laugh as young men usually did, but their faces were grave, as they talked of the foreign lands, the war, their country, the big unemployment and the stolen lands.

Njoroge listened keenly as they talked of Jomo. Already he felt intimate with this man. For Njoroge was sure that he had read about him in the Old Testament. Moses had led the children of Israel from Misri to the Promised Land. And because black people were really the children of Israel, Moses was no other than Jomo himself. It was obvious.

The men also talked of the strike. All men who worked for white men and Serikali (the Government) would come out on strike. The Government and the settlers had to be shown that black people were not cowards and slaves. They too had children to feed and to educate. How could people go on sweating

50

for the children of the white men to be well-fed, well-clothed and well-educated? Kiarie, a short man with a black beard, was a good, compelling speaker. He usually walked together with Boro. His words stirred Njoroge strangely.

A man asked, 'But do you think it will succeed?'

'Yes! Everybody will go on strike. Every black man everywhere. Even those in the police and the army will sit down too.'

'Shall we really get the same pay as Indians and Europeans?'

'Yes!' Kiarie explained with a confident nod of his head. 'All the black people will stop working. All business in the country will come to a standstill because all the country depends on our sweat. The Government and the settlers will call us back. But we shall say, No, no. Give us more money first. Our sweat and blood are not so cheap. We too are human beings. We cannot live on fifteen shillings a month. . . .'

The old men and village folk listened with deep interest. They did not know much about strikes but if this meant more money it was a good idea. The solemn voice of Kiarie had conviction and quiet assurance, which, Njoroge felt, gave courage and faith to all those around.

'What about those employed by black people?'

'We must concentrate on the Government and the white people. We black people are brothers.'

Ngotho knew of one or two who were certainly *not* brothers. But he did not say so.

When Njoroge went to bed, he prayed that the strike be a success. He hoped it would come soon. If his father had much money, he could buy a lorry like that one of Jacobo. He slept and dreamed of the happy moment of wealth and pleasure after the strike.

Mr Howlands called all his men. This was unusual. But he had not much to say because he did not want to waste time. He just warned them that if any man went on strike he would instantly lose his job. How could he allow a damned strike to interfere with any part of his farm? Even the Government could not interfere with this. The blacks could ask and agitate for anything. Such things were clearly affairs of the Government – affairs that stood outside his *shamba*. And yet paradoxically, as the strike approached, he wanted a strong government action – an action that would teach these labourers their rightful places.

Ngotho listened to the warning without apparent emotion. His face did not change and so you could not tell what he was really thinking.

He could not quite make up his mind about the strike. He doubted if the strike would be a success. If it failed, then he would lose a job and that would keep him away from the lands of his ancestors. This was wrong, for the land was his. None could tend it as he could.

Ngotho went home unsure. He went through the African shops. The barber was still at his job. These days he mostly talked about the strike. Ngotho did not go there. He went straight home.

Njoroge had never seen his father quarrelling with his wives. Whenever there was a quarrel, the children were never allowed to know about it. So when Njoroge came from school and found Nyokabi crying, he was shocked. He could remember vaguely only one time when his mother cried. It was probably during the famine of cassava or earlier. That was now a dream. But this was not a dream. Njoroge stood stock still, too frightened to enter the house. Ngotho, tall, masculine in spite of age, stood in front of her. Njoroge could not see his face. But he could see the tear-washed face of Nyokabi. Fear gripped him as he witnessed real discord in the home that had hitherto been so secure.

'I must be a man in my own house.'

'Yes – be a man and lose a job.'

'I shall do whatever I like. I have never taken orders from a woman.'

'We shall starve. . . .'

'You starve! This strike is important for the black people. We shall get bigger salaries.'

'What's black people to us when we starve?'

'Shut that mouth. How long do you think I can endure this drudgery, for the sake of a white man and his children?'

'But he's paying you money. What if the strike fails?'

'Don't woman me!' he shouted hysterically. This possibility was what he feared most. She sensed this note of uncertainty and fear and seized upon it.

'What if the strike fails, tell me that!'

Ngotho could bear it no longer. She was driving him mad. He slapped her on the face and raised his hand again. But Njoroge now found his voice. He ran forward and cried frantically, 'Please, father.'

Ngotho stopped. He looked at his son. He ran towards him and grabbed him by the shoulder. Njoroge felt the grip and winced with fear. Ngotho growled something inaudible. Then he suddenly released the boy and turned his eyes away. He walked out.

'Mother!' Njoroge whispered to Nyokabi.

'Why have they bewitched him? My man is changed. . . .'

'Please, mother!'

But she went on sobbing.

Njoroge felt lonely. Something heavy and cold oppressed him in the stomach. Even the stars that later shone in the night gave him no comfort. He walked across the courtyard, not afraid of the darkness. He wished that Mwihaki was with him. Then he might have confided in her. In the distance, the gleaming lights of the city where the call for the strike had been born beckoned to him. He did not respond. He just wanted to be lost in the darkness for he could not judge between a father and mother.

In his bed, he knelt down and prayed. 'God forgive me for I am wicked. Perhaps it is me who has brought uncleanliness into our home. Forgive me my sins. Help my father and mother. O, God of Abraham, Isaac and Jacobo, help Thy children. Forgive us all. Amen.

'Lord, do you think the strike will be a success?'

He wanted an assurance. He wanted a foretaste of the future before it came. In the Old Testament, God spoke to His people. Surely He could do the same thing now. So Njoroge listened, seriously and quietly. He was still listening when he fell asleep.

CHAPTER SEVEN

It was at the beginning of New Year. The room was packed, for the whole class had come to know whether they had passed or not. Njoroge sat in a corner, silent. Mwihaki too was there. She was growing into quite a big girl; certainly she was not the same person who five years back had taken Njoroge to school. The two had shared each other's hopes and fears and he felt akin to her. He always wished she had been his sister. A boy chattered and shouted in a corner, but his friend did not want to play. The boy sat down again while the two others regarded him coldly. One or two others laughed. But the laughter was rather subdued. Though they sat in groups, each was alone. That was all.

Teacher Isaka came in with a long sheet of paper. Everybody kept quiet. Njoroge had prepared himself for this moment. He had many times told himself that he would not change even if he failed. He had tried his best. But now when the teacher began to look at the long white sheet, he wanted to go and hide under the desk. And then he heard his name. It was topping the list. Mwihaki too had passed.

Together they ran homewards linking their hands. They did not talk. Each wanted to reach home and tell their parents the good news. Njoroge wanted his mother to know that her son had not failed. He would now go to an intermediate school. They came near Mwihaki's house and there stood for a moment holding each other's hands. Then they let go the hands and each now ran on a different path towards home.

Mwihaki reached home earlier. She found her mother and all the other children of the family crowded together. She did not see anything strange in this because she was very excited.

'Mother! Mother!'

'What is it?' She stopped. The voice of her mother was cold, sad and distant. Juliana looked past Mwihaki and then, almost in a hostile and impatient manner continued, 'What else has happened? Speak! or why do you come home rushing so?'

'Nothing,' Mwihaki said quietly, 'only that I have passed.' There was no pride of achievement in her voice.

'Is that all? Is your sister Lucia at school?'

Then Juliana burst out sobbing, speaking to herself. 'I have always said that such *Ahoi* were dangerous. But a man will never heed the voice of a woman until it is too late. I told him not to go. But he would not listen!'

'What has happened, mother?' Mwihaki asked anxiously.

'O, well may you ask. I've always said that your father will end up by being murdered!'

'Is he dead?' Mwihaki burst out crying.

Nobody reassured her.

Meanwhile Njoroge had reached home. A group of men and women and children were standing in the courtyard. Some eyes were turned to his father's hut. The others were turned towards the market place. But where was his mother? He found her inside her hut. She sat on a low stool and two women of the village sat close to her. They kept dumb. Their eyes were turned to the courtyard. Nyokabi's face was dark and now and then sobs shook her. Njoroge's joy of a victorious homecoming faded.

'What is it, mother?' He feared that someone had died.

His mother looked up and saw him. Njoroge trembled. Outside more men and women streamed into the courtyard. Some spoke in low voices.

'It's the strike!' A woman told him. And then, of course, Njoroge remembered. Today was the great day of the strike – the strike that was meant to paralyse the whole country.

Many people had gone to the meeting which was being held on the first day of the strike. They had streamed into the meeting ground like safari ants. All knew that this was a great day for the black people. Ngotho too had gone to the meeting. Who could tell but that the meeting might open the door to better things? And would it have paid to have been in Howlands' employment when the time for the settlement of things came? That was how he comforted himself because Nyokabi's words were still in his mind. The barber came and sat next to him. All the time, the barber kept up an incessant chatter that made people laugh. The speakers had come from Nairobi and among them were Boro and Kiarie. Boro had not found a permanent job in Nairobi but had gone into politics. Ngotho felt a certain pride in seeing his son sitting with such big folk. He was now glad that he had come.

Kiarie spoke first, in a low, sad voice and recounted history. All the land belonged to the people – black people. They had been given it by God. For every race had their country. The Indians had India. Europeans had Europe. And Africans had Africa, the land of the black people. (*Applause*) Who did not know that all the soil in this part of the country had been given to Gikuyu and Mumbi and their posterity? (*More applause*) He told them how the land had been taken away, through the Bible and the sword. 'Yes, that's how your land was taken away. The Bible paved the way for the sword.' For this, he blamed the foolish generosity of their forefathers who pitied the stranger and welcomed him with open arms into their fold.

'Later, our fathers were taken captives in the first Big War to help in a war whose cause they never knew. And when they came back? Their land had been taken away for a settlement of the white soldiers. Was that fair? (*No!*) Our people were taken and forced to work for these settlers. How could they have done otherwise when their land had been taken and they and their wives were required to pay heavy taxes to a government that was not theirs? When people rose to demand their rights they were shot down. But still the Serikali and settlers were not satisfied. When the second Big War came, we were taken to fight Hitler – Hitler who had not wronged us. We were killed, we shed blood to save the British Empire from defeat and collapse.' God had now heard their cries and tribulations. There was a man sent from God whose name was Jomo. He was the Black Moses empowered by God to tell the white Pharaoh 'Let my people go!'

'And that's what we have gathered here to tell the British. Today, we, with one voice, we must rise and shout: "The time has come. Let my People go. Let my People go! We want back our land! Now!" ' (*Hysterical applause*)

Ngotho had felt a hollow strife in his stomach. It fixed him to the ground so that he could not applaud. He looked from the ground and saw the shouting and applauding figures. But he saw everything in a mist. He saw blurred images. Was he crying? The images around transformed themselves from something grey to blue and then to total black. They were black sweaters. He cleared his eyes. The black sweaters remained there, now approaching. And then he saw. He was not in a dream. The police had surrounded the whole meeting.

Kiarie was now speaking in a loud voice –

'Remember, this must be a peaceful strike. We must get more pay. Because right is on our side we shall triumph. If today, you're hit, don't hit back. . . .' A white police inspector had got up on to the platform. And with him – *Jacobo!* At first Ngotho could not understand. It was all strange. It was only when Jacobo had begun to speak and was urging people to go back to work and not listen to some people from Nairobi who had nothing to lose if people lost their jobs that Ngotho understood. Jacobo, the richest man in all the land around, had been brought to pacify the people. Everyone listened to him in silence. But something unusual happened to Ngotho. For one single moment Jacobo crystallized into a concrete betrayal of the people. He became the physical personification of the long years of waiting and suffering – Jacobo was a Traitor. Ngotho rose. He made his way towards the platform while everyone watched, wondering what was happening. He was now near Jacobo. The battle was now between these two – Jacobo on the side of the white people and he on the side of the black people.

All this happened quickly and took the people by surprise. And then all of a sudden, as if led by Ngotho, the crowd rose and rushed towards Jacobo. At once the police acted, throwing tear-gas bombs and firing into the crowd, and two men fell as the panic-stricken mob scattered. Ngotho's courage now failed him. He was lost in the crowd. So he ran blindly, not knowing whither. He wanted only to save his life. A policeman struck at his face with a baton and drew blood. But he did not stop. He was not really aware of the blood, he felt it only as something warm. Frantically he ran until he was in the clear, then stumbled forward and fell, losing consciousness. That was where people from his village found him, the hero of the hour, and took him home.

'Is he going to die?' Njoroge asked Kamau after hearing the story.

'No! It is not very serious. But I think he lost much blood.'

'Why did he do it, I mean, attack Jacobo?'

'I don't know. We just saw him rise and when near Jacobo, he turned round and shouted to all of us "Arise". I think he was mad with emotion. But then so were we all. I didn't know that father could have such a voice.'

A small silence fell between them. Kamau seemed to be recollecting the scene. Some men and women were beginning to move from the courtyard.

'Why did Jacobo do that?'

'He is an enemy of the black people. He doesn't want others to be as rich as he is.'

How had Jacobo become involved? That was a question that few could answer with much certainty. Few knew that to the Government and the settlers around, Jacobo, being a rich man, had a lot of influence on the people. Jacobo had of course impressed this on the local white community, including Mr

Howlands, who had not taken him seriously until the hour of need. Jacobo was a convenient man. The police had called him to their aid and Jacobo could not have refused. For a time he had thought himself successful. Then this damned Ngotho had come and spoilt everything.

Jacobo was not seriously hurt. The police had acted in time. Otherwise he would have been torn to pieces. While it lasted, it had been like death itself. He wished he had listened to the voice of his wife.

At the barber's shop was a large crowd of people. The barber who had sat next to Ngotho was retelling the whole incident. This was a few days after the affair.

'The old man is brave.'

'He is that, to be sure.'

'Was he badly hurt?'

'No, except that much blood came out.'

'Why did he do it? His action caused the death of two men.'

'Ah, who could not have done as he did! I sat next to him, and I would have done the same thing. It would have been all right if it had been a white man, but a black man – like you and me! It shows that we black people will never be united. There must always be a traitor in our midst.'

'That's true, that's true!' several voices agreed.

'There be some people everywhere who don't want to see others rise—' the young man who was being trimmed put in.

Then the barber took up, 'You have said the truth. Jacobo is rich. You all know that he was the first black man to be allowed to grow pyrethrum. Do you think he would like to see another one near him? And how, anyway, do you think he was allowed what had been denied the rest?' No one could answer. Then the barber stopped the machine for a while. In a wise manner, he declared. 'It's because he promised them to sell us.'

'Yes! Yes!' Again several voices agreed. A middle-aged man with a bald head sadly shook his head and said, 'All the same, it's sad what has happened to Ngotho. He has been told to leave Jacobo's land.'

'Leave Jacobo's land?'

'Y-e-e-s!'

'But Jacobo found him there when he bought the land from the previous owner.'

'It is his land. He can do what he likes with it.'

The man who said this was a modern young man who had just joined the group. People turned on him angrily.

'But is it not against the custom? Besides the previous owner never actually sold the sites to Jacobo. . . .'

A policeman was seen in the distance. The crowd quickly dispersed. The barber was left alone. By now many people knew that the strike had failed.

Ngotho was given a place to build by Nganga. It was then that Njoroge realized that the man's rough exterior and apparent lack of scruple concealed a warm heart. His old hatred of Nganga vanished. Even Kamau could now speak of him with enthusiasm.

But all this was a hard period for Njoroge. New huts meant more money being spent and Ngotho had lost his job in the settled area. Fees had risen for those who went to Standard V in the new school. Besides, there was the building fund to be paid. The new school would soon be built with stone. Njoroge had no money. Mwihaki had gone to a boarding school for girls far away. She would go on with learning, but he, Njoroge, would stop. This hurt him. Day by day, he prayed. What would he do to realize his vision? On the Monday of the third week, he was sent home. On the way he cried.

God heard his prayers. Kamau's wages had been raised to thirty shillings. This he gave to Njoroge. The rest was made up by Kori. Njoroge was glad. He would go on with learning.

INTERLUDE

Exactly two and a half years later, on a certain hill over-looking Nairobi, there stood a disillusioned government official. He was all alone, looking at the country he would soon be leaving.

Why do you stand there amazed?

I did not know that this would come to be.

But you saw the signs?

No. I didn't.

You did.

I didn't!

But—

I tell you I didn't. We tried our best.

He walked away, stamping his feet angrily on the ground.

'And to think of all we did for them,' he said. The dumb city he and others of his kind had helped to create looked at him. There was no comfort from that corner, the very centre of the trouble.

'Have you heard, brother?'

'No!'

'But you have not asked me what.'

'My children cry for food.'

'But don't you want to hear what happened in Murang'a?'

'Oh, Murang'a. That's far away. . . .'

'A chief has been killed.'

'Oh! Is that all? My wife is waiting for me.'

'But it's all interesting—'

'I'll come, then, in the evening for the story.'

'All right. Do. Other people are coming. I have a wireless set.'

'My wife calls. Stay in peace.'
'Go in peace.'

'He was a big chief.'
'Like Jacobo?'
'No. Bigger. He used to eat with the Governor.'
'Was he actually killed in daylight?'
'Yes. The men were very daring.'
'Tell us it all again.'
'Woman, add more wood to the fire and light the lantern, for darkness falls. . . . Now, the chief was a big man with much land. The Governor had given it all to him, so he might sell the black people. The men were in a car. The chief was also in a car. The two men followed him all the way from Nairobi. When they reached the countryside, the men drove ahead and waved the chief to stop. He stopped. "Who's the chief?" "I am." "Then take *that* and *that*. And *that* too." They shot him dead and drove away—'
'In daylight?'
'In daylight. The man on the wireless said so.'
'This generation.'
'Very daring. They have learned the trick from the white man.'
'It's almost time for news. Let's hear what the man will say—'
'Hush!'

One night people heard that Jomo and all the leaders of the land were arrested. A state of emergency had been declared.
'But they cannot arrest Jomo,' said the barber.
'They cannot.'
'They want to leave people without a leader.'
'Yes. They are after oppressing us,' said the barber. He did not speak with the usual lively tone.
'What's a state of emergency?' a man asked.
'Oh, don't ask a foolish question. Haven't you heard about Malaya?'

'What about it?'

'There was a state of emergency.'

Njoroge was a little annoyed when he heard about Jomo's arrest. He had cherished the idea of seeing this man who had become famous all over Kenya. He could still remember a meeting arranged in the market place by K.A.U. It was many months after the strike that failed. K.A.U. was the society of black people who wanted *Wiyathi* and the return of the stolen lands. The society also wanted bigger salaries for black people and the abolition of colour-bar. Njoroge had heard about the colour-bar from his brothers in Nairobi. He did not know what it was really. But he knew that the strike had failed because of the colour-bar. Black people had no land because of colour-bar and they could not eat in hotels because of colour-bar. Colour-bar was everywhere. Rich Africans could also practise colour-bar on the poorer Africans. . . .

Njoroge had gone early to the market place. But he had found that many people had already reached the place and blocked his view. All right, he would see him next time.

But now Jomo had been arrested.

PART TWO

DARKNESS FALLS

CHAPTER EIGHT

One heard stories about what was happening in Nyeri and Murang'a. Nyeri and Murang'a were far from Njoroge's home. The stories that he heard were interesting and some boys could tell them well. Njoroge listened carefully and wondered how boys like Karanja had come to know so many stories.

'Tell us more.'

'Yes. What happened next?'

'You see he had written a letter to the police station at Nyeri. "I, Dedan Kimathi, Leader of the African Freedom Army, will come to visit you at 10.30 a.m. on Sunday." Many more police were called from Nairobi to strengthen the force at Nyeri. Curfew was extended to daytime so that no one could leave his home. Every soldier was on the alert so that when Dedan came he could easily be arrested. At 10.30 then, on that very Sunday, a white police inspector on a big old motor-bike came to the police post. He was tall, smartly dressed, but very fierce-looking. Every policeman stood at attention. He inspected them all and wished them good luck in catching Dedan. After he had finished, he told them that his motor-bike was not working well. Could they give him another one as he was in a hurry to get down to Nairobi? They did. He rode away on a new motor-bike. The police still waited for Dedan.'

'Did he come?'

'Don't interrupt. Please Karanja, go on.' Several voices cried.

'Well, they did not see anyone else that Sunday. They were all annoyed. On the following day, they got a letter which was actually dropped by a flying aeroplane.'

'What was in the letter?'

Karanja looked at them all in a lordly, knowing manner. Then he slowly said, 'The letter came from Dedan.'

'Haaa!'

'In it he thanked the police because they had waited for him and had given him a better motor-bike.'

'You mean the police inspector had actually been Dedan himself?'

'Yes.'

'But that one was white?'

'That's the point. Dedan can change himself into anything – a white man, a bird, or a tree. He can also turn himself into an aeroplane. He learnt all this in the Big War.'

Njoroge left school. He had now been in this new school for two years. In spite of difficulties at home he had managed to go on. With equal good luck he would eventually get what he wanted. He went home thinking about Karanja's story. He knew that it was exaggerated but still there might be an element of truth in it. Stranger things had been said to happen. He had heard his father and Kamau say that Kimathi could do very wonderful things. He must surely be a great man to elude all the keen vigilance of the white man.

He reached home. The three huts put up hurriedly stood before him. This was his new home – his home since they were asked to quit Jacobo's land. They had been years of struggle, with Ngotho without a job and Boro much more changed and withdrawn than ever. Had it not been for Kori and Kamau he did not know what they could have done. Jacobo had now been made a chief. He moved with one or two policemen always by his side, carrying guns to protect him against the *Ihii cia mutitu* (Freedom Boys of the Forest). The Chief went from one hut to the next checking and patrolling. Sometimes he went around with the new District Officer. The new D.O. was actually Mr Howlands himself.

A small bush hid the courtyard from immediate view. Behind him the land of Nganga, their new landlord, sloped gently merging with some tall gum trees farther down. Njoroge was tired for his new school was five miles away from home.

And he had to do all that journey on foot. This was what education meant to thousands of boys and girls in all the land. Schools were scarce and very widely spaced. Independent and Kikuyu Karing'a schools, which had been built by the people after a break with the missions, had been closed by the Government, and this made the situation worse. There was nobody in the courtyard. The sun had already set and the usual evening breeze that came between sunset and total darkness was absent. The whole land looked deceptively calm. Njoroge stood for a moment, made uneasy by this quiet atmosphere that preceded darkness. At first he did not hear anything. Then he strained his ears and heard a murmur of voices in Njeri's hut. It was very cold and dark. There was no sign of food anywhere and he became colder and more hungry.

He went to Njeri's hut.

The whole family was gathered there. Njoroge saw the dark face of his father. His face always wore something akin to a frown ever since that strike. Behind him was Kamau, who stood leaning against a post. Farther on, hidden in a shadowy corner and sitting on a bed, were his two mothers. Njoroge went right in and the gloom in the room caught him at once.

'Sit down!' Ngotho quietly ordered him. It was unnecessary for Njoroge was already preparing to sit down. As he sat he turned his eyes to the left. There, hidden by a shadow from the small wall that partitioned the hut, was his brother, Boro. For many months Boro had not been seen at home.

'Oh, I'm sorry. How is it with you?'

'It's well, brother. How is school?' Boro had always shown a marked interest in Njoroge's progress at school.

'It's all well. How's Nairobi? I hope you left Kori in peace.'

'O, dear child, we hope he's well!' It was his father who answered him. Njoroge fearfully looked at Boro. There was silence.

Njeri said, 'Do you think he is safe?'

'I don't know. He is not alone. There are many more with him.'

'So you don't know where the others were taken. . . .'

'That's right.' He kept on looking at the ground and then rose up unsteadily. He was a little excited. Then he sat down again and almost in a crying voice said, 'If they should, oh, if—'

Njoroge thought Boro was mad. But just at that moment, the door opened and Kori staggered in. He wore a haggard, haunted look. He almost fell down.

'What is it?' the two women spoke together.

'Water and food,' he gasped. After a while he related his story to his surprised audience. But he first laughed.

'Many, many will be in prison. What a waste!' Then he turned to his brother. 'So you are one of the three who escaped?'

'We were five.'

'They said you were terrorists.'

'How did you—?'

'After they took us to the field, I lost you. Then you escaped, and the police became more vigilant and even beat some people. Before daybreak, we were put into trucks. We did not know where we were being taken. I feared that we might be killed. This feeling became stronger when we came to a forest and the truck in which I was slowed down. I immediately got the idea that I should jump, which I did. They were taken by surprise and before they could fire, I had vanished into the forest. Look at my knee—'

They crowded around him – all except Boro who remained wrapped in thought. The knee was tied with a dirty piece of cloth and when he removed it, they could see where the sands had eaten in.

'Ha, ha! I've no idea if they went to look for me. For days I've been travelling like you, only I got a lift by a lorry-driver.'

'Why do they oppress the black people?' Njeri bitterly

70

asked. She was growing old. Her days of poverty and hardship were being made heavier by this anxiety. But just now her heart was a little lighter.

They talked in whispers far into the night.

'They want to oppress people before Jomo comes out. They know he'll win the case. That's why they are afraid,' Kori was explaining.

'Will they let all those in detention free if he wins?'

'Oh, yes. All of them. And *Wiyathi* will come.'

Ngotho did not speak much. He sat in his own corner and Njoroge could not tell if he was listening to what was going on. Ngotho was changing. Soon after the strike Boro quarrelled much with the old man. He accused him of having spoilt everything by his rash action in spite of Kiarie's warning. Boro clearly had contempt for Ngotho. But he had never expressed it in words except on those two occasions. Since then, he had become more critical of Ngotho. Ngotho, as a result, had diminished in stature, often assuming a defensive secondary place whenever talking with his sons and their friends. For months he had remained in this position, often submitting unflinchingly to his son. And then Boro thought that he could make the old man submit to his will. But Ngotho made a determined resistance. He would not take the Mau Mau oath at his son's hands or instruction. There had been a bitter quarrel and Boro had stayed for a long time without coming home.

CHAPTER NINE

Everyone knew that Jomo would win. God would not let His people alone. The children of Israel must win. Many people put all their hopes on this eventual victory. If he lost, then the black people of Kenya had lost. Some of his lawyers had even come from England.

Much rain fell at Kipanga and the country around on the eve of the judgement day. People were happy in all the land. The rain was a good omen. Black folk were on trial. The spirit of black folk from Demi na Mathathi was on trial. Would it be victorious? It was the growing uncertainty of the answer that made people be afraid and assert more and more aggressively that a victory would surely follow.

At school a little argument ensued. It was begun by Karanja. Karanja came from Ndeiya next to the Masai country. He said, 'Jomo is bound to win. Europeans fear him.'

'No. He can't win. My father said so last night.'

'Your father is a homeguard,' another boy retorted. The two boys began a quarrel. Another discussion arose somewhere else.

'The homeguards with their white masters. They are as bad as Mau Mau.'

'No. Mau Mau is not bad. The Freedom boys are fighting against white settlers. Is it bad to fight for one's land? Tell me that.'

'But they cut black men's throats.'

'Those killed are the traitors! Black white settlers.'

'What's Mau Mau?' Njoroge asked. He had never known what it was and his curiosity overcame his fear of being thought ignorant.

Karanja, who had just joined the group, said, 'It is a secret Kiama. You "drink" oath. You become a member. The Kiama has its own soldiers who are fighting for the land. Kimathi is the leader.'

'Not Jomo?' a small boy with one bad eye asked.

'I don't know,' Karanja continued. 'But father says that Kimathi is the leader of the Freedom Army and Jomo is the leader of K.A.U. I like K.A.U. and fear Mau Mau.'

'But they are all the same? Fighting for the freedom of the black people.' This was said by a tall but weak boy. Then with a distant look in his eyes, 'I would like to fight in the forest.'

All eyes were turned on him. He seemed to have said a very profound thing. Or seemed to have put in words what most of them felt. A solemn air hung over all the group. Then one other boy broke the silence by saying, 'I too would like to fight. I would love to carry a big gun like my father used to do in the Big War when he fought for the British. Now I would be fighting for the black folk—'

'Hurrah and victory for the black folk!'

'Hurrah and victory for Jomo—'

'It rained last night.'

The bell went, the group dispersed. They rushed back for their evening classes.

That night Njoroge learnt that Jomo lost. His spirit fell and he felt something queer in his stomach. He did not know what to think.

'But it was all arranged,' Kori explained. They all gathered in Njeri's hut, now together only for comfort. In the morning people would not say *Kwa Heri* (goodbye) at parting for fear of contemplating what such a farewell might imply. It might mean 'For ever, farewell'. Ngotho himself lived in fear for his family because Jacobo who had now become the most powerful man in the land had never forgiven him. He knew that sooner or later the Chief would retaliate. Perhaps he was biding his time. What did he live for now? His days were full of weariness. He had no longer *the waiting* to sustain him. The fulfilment of the prophecy seemed to be impossible. Perhaps he had blundered in going on strike. For he had now lost every contact with his ancestral land. The communion with the spirits who had gone before him had given him vitality. But what could he have done? He had to go on strike. He had not wanted to be accused by a son any more because when a man was accused by the eyes of his son who had been to war and had witnessed the death of a brother he felt guilty. But Ngotho had always wanted to be gentle with Boro because he knew that the son must have been sorely tried in the war. The *something* that had urged him to fight against Jacobo certainly had no logic. But it alienated Boro further still. Ngotho often wondered if he had really done well by his sons. If he and his generation had failed, he was ready to suffer for it. . . . But whatever Ngotho had been prepared to do to redeem himself in the eyes of his children, he would not be ordered by a son to take oath. Not that he objected to it in principle. After all, oath-taking as a means of binding a person to a promise was a normal feature of tribal life. But to be given by a son! That would have violated against his standing as a father. A lead in that direction could only come from him, the head of the family. Not from a son; not even if he had been to many places and knew many things. That gave him no right to reverse the custom and tradition for which he and those of his generation stood. And yet he felt the loss of the land even more keenly than Boro, for to him it was a spiritual loss. When a man was severed from the land of his ancestors where would he sacrifice to the Creator? How could he come into contact with the founder of the tribe, Gikuyu and Mumbi? What did Boro know of oaths, of ancient rites, of the spirits of the ancestors? Still the estrangement cut deeper and deeper into Ngotho's life, emaciating him daily.

To him, too, Jomo had been his hope. Ngotho had come to think that it was Jomo who would drive away the white men. To him Jomo stood for custom and tradition purified by grace of learning and much travel. But now he was defeated. Things had clearly gone against him in his old age; Jacobo, a chief, and Howlands, a D.O. And now he was also estranged from a son of his own skin and blood. Could he now put his faith in the youngest of the sons? But did Njoroge understand what was happening? But then who understood anything anyway?

Again tonight they spoke in whispers. Boro sat in his own corner and seemed more withdrawn than ever.

'It was to be expected,' Kori said again.

Nyokabi said, 'I knew he would lose. I always said that all white men are the same. His lawyers must have been bribed.'

'It is more than that,' said Njeri. 'And although I am a woman and cannot explain it, it seems all clear as daylight. The white man makes a law or a rule. Through that rule or law or what you may call it, he takes away the land and then imposes many laws on the people concerning that land and many other things, all without people agreeing first as in the old days of the tribe. Now a man rises and opposes that law which made right the taking away of land. Now that man is taken by the same people who made the laws against which that man was fighting. He is tried under those alien rules. Now tell me who is that man who can win even if the angels of God were his lawyers ... I mean.'

Njeri was panting. Njoroge had never heard her speak for such a long time. Yet there seemed to be something in what she had said. Everyone looked at her. Tears were on her face. Boro was now speaking. But it was a lamentation.

'... All white people stick together. But we black people are very divided. And because they stick together, they've imprisoned Jomo, the only hope we had. Now they'll make us slaves. They took us to their wars and they killed all that was of value to us. ...' Njoroge convulsively clutched the seat more firmly with his hands. All the wrong done to the people was concentrated in the plaintive voice of Boro. Njoroge felt ready to do anything to right those wrongs. But inside himself he was afraid.

All of a sudden, Boro stood and almost shouted,

'Never! never! Black people must rise up and fight.'

Njoroge's eyes dilated. Nyokabi held her breath while Njeri turned her eyes fearfully towards the door.

CHAPTER TEN

The office was a small rectangular building with a roof of red tiles. But around the main office were other buildings some made of stone and corrugated iron roofs. A small village of huts built of grass thatched roofs and white-washed mud walls completed the whole police garrison. Around the garrison was a fence of barbed wire.

Mr Howlands sat in the office with his left elbow on the table with the palm of the hand supporting his head. He held a pencil in his right hand with which he kept on tapping the table while he gazed out through the small open glass window with a strained expression. Looking at him, one would have thought that he was gazing at the huts that made the police quarters. His mind was far away back into his childhood, in the small rectangular hedge outside his home and the boys with whom he used to play. The joys, fears, and hopes of childhood were grand in their own way. The little quarrels he had had; the father whom he had feared and revered; the gentle mother in whose arms he could always find solace and comfort – all these at times assaulted his memory, especially in these troubled times. And yet these were the things he had all along wanted to shut from his life.

He stood and walked across the office, wrapped in thought. He now knew maybe there was no escape. The present that had made him a D.O. reflected a past from which he had tried to run away. That past had followed him even though he had tried to avoid politics, government, and anything else that might remind him of that betrayal. But his son had been taken away. ... It was no good calling on the name of God for he, Howlands, did not believe in God. There was only one god for him – and that was the farm he had created, the land he had tamed.

And who were these Mau Mau who were now claiming that land, his god? Ha, ha! He could have laughed at the whole ludicrous idea, but for the fact that they had forced him into the other life, the life he had tried to avoid. He had been called upon to take up a temporary appointment as a District Officer. He had agreed. But only because this meant defending his god. If Mau Mau claimed the only thing he believed in, they would see! Did they want to drive him back to England, the forgotten land? They were mistaken. Who were black men and Mau Mau anyway, he asked for the thousandth time? Mere savages! A nice word – savages. Previously he had not thought of them as savages or otherwise, simply because he had not thought of them at all, except as a part of the farm – the way one thought of donkeys or horses in his farm except that in the case of donkeys and horses one had to think of their food and a place for them to sleep. The strike which had made him lose Ngotho and now brought about the emergency had forced him to think, to move out of his shell. But they all would pay for this! Yes, he would wring from every single man the last drop till they had all been reduced to nothingness, till he had won a victory for his god. The Mau Mau had come to symbolize all that which he had tried to put aside in life. To conquer it would give him a spiritual satisfaction, the same sort of satisfaction he had got from the conquest of his land. He was like a lion that was suddenly woken from his lair.

He looked at his watch. It looked small on his wrist. He was expecting the Chief. Mr Howlands despised Jacobo because he was a savage. But he would use him. The very ability to set these people fighting amongst themselves instead of fighting with the white men gave him an amused satisfaction.

He sat down again and began to think of home – his home. He wondered what he would do with his son Stephen. He did not want to send him to that England, even though his wife was daily urging him to let them go till things were normal again. To submit to his wife was to listen to the voice of England. No. He would not give in to either Mau Mau or his wife. He would reduce everything to his will. That was the settlers' way. It was odd that he should only think of his wife and child Stephen. The truth was that his daughter did not quite exist for him. She had thwarted his will and desire and had gone to be a missionary. What did she want to be a missionary for? Even the attempt to explain on his daughter's side had only served to exasperate him the more. She had given herself wholly to God and to His eternal service.

There was a knock at the door. Jacobo, gun in hand, came in. He removed his hat and folded it respectfully. There was a big grin which Howlands hated. He had known him for quite a long time. Jacobo had occasionally come to him for advice. Howlands had always given it while he talked of what he had done and what he would do with the land he had tamed. Howlands had in fact helped Jacobo to get permission to grow pyrethrum. In turn Jacobo had helped him to recruit labour and gave him advice on how to get hard work from them. However all this had been a part of the farm. Duty had now thrown them together and he could now see Jacobo in a new light.

'Sit down, Jacobo.'

'Thank you, sir.'

'What did you want to see me for?'

'Well, sir, it's a long affair.'

'Make it short.'

'Yes, sir. As I was telling you the other day, I keep an eye on everybody in the village. Now this man Ngotho, as you know, is a bad man. A very terrible man. He has taken many oaths.' It looked as if Howlands was not attending so Jacobo paused for a while. Then he beamed. 'You know, he is the one who led the strike.'

'I know,' Howlands cut in. 'What has he done?'

'Well, as I was telling you, it is a long affair. You know this man has sons. These sons of his had been away from the village for quite a long time. I think they are bringing trouble in the village. ... I am very suspicious about Boro, the eldest son.

Now this man, sir, had been to the war and I think, sir, he was connected with the strike—'

'Yes! yes! What have they done?'

'I, well, sir, nothing, but you see these people work in secret. I was just thinking that we should sort of remove them from the village . . . send them to one of the detention camps. . . . Now, if we leave them alone, there'll flare up big, big trouble in the village. Their detention would make it easier to keep an eye on this Ngotho because as I was telling you he may be the real leader of Mau Mau.'

'All right. Just keep an eye on the sons. Arrest them for anything, curfew, tax, you know what.'

'Yes sir.'

'Anything else?'

'Nothing, sir.'

'All right. You can go.'

'Thank you, sir, thank you. I think this Mau Mau will be beaten.'

Howlands did not answer.

'Good-bye sir.'

'All right,' Howlands roughly said as he stood up as if to show the Chief out.

Mr Howlands watched him go out. Then he banged the door and stood by the small window. He had never forgotten Ngotho.

Ngotho and his family sat in Nyokabi's hut. These days people sat late only in families. Two were missing from the family group. Kamau was in the African market. He preferred staying and even sleeping there. He felt it safer that way. Boro was not in. He would probably be late. They sat in darkness. Lights had to be put out early. And they spoke in whispers, although they did not speak much. They had little to say except make irrelevant remarks here and a joke there at which nobody laughed. They knew the dark night would be long. Boro and Kori kept their beds in Njeri's hut. Her hut was a few yards away from Nyokabi's. Njeri and Kori waited for Boro to turn up but when he failed they rose up to go. Perhaps Boro would come later in the night or he could sleep wherever he was. Who would dare to go home on such a night, and there being curfew order for everyone to be in by six o'clock? They went out. No good night. The others remained. All of a sudden there was a shout that split the night—

'Halt:'

Njoroge trembled. He would not go to the door where his father and mother stood looking at whatever was happening outside. He remained rooted to the seat. His father came back from the door and sat heavily on the stool he had quickly vacated when he had heard the order for Njeri, his wife, and Kori, his son, to stop. Nyokabi later came in. She lit the lantern and seeing the face of Ngotho put it out again. Silence reigned.

'They have taken them away,' Nyokabi sobbed. Njoroge felt as if there were some invisible dark shapes in the hut.

At last Ngotho said, 'Yeees. . . .' His voice was unsteady. He felt like crying, but the humiliation and pain he felt had a stunning effect. Was he a *man* any longer, he who had watched his wife and son taken away because of breaking the curfew without a word of protest? Was this cowardice? It was cowardice, cowardice of the worst sort. He stood up and rushed to the door like a madman. It was too late. He came back to his seat, a defeated man, a man who cursed himself for being a man with a lost manhood. He now knew that even that waiting had been a form of cowardice, a putting off of action.

He now quietly said, 'I know it is Jacobo.'

Again Njoroge held on to a stool to keep himself steady. It was the first time that any member of his family had been caught by the new laws, although Boro, Kori and Kamau had always had narrow escapes, especially during the police operations. What was now happening to his father and what would happen to Kori and Njeri?

'Jacobo wants to ruin me. He wants to destroy this house. He will do it.'

80

It was a kind of defiant lamentation that was worse than a violent outburst of anger.

At that minute Boro entered. Again silence reigned till Boro broke it by asking what was wrong.

'They have taken your mother and brother away,' Ngotho said, his head still bowed.

'They have taken my mother and brother away!' Boro slowly repeated.

'Yes. Curfew,' Nyokabi said. She hastily stole a glance at Boro. She was glad that the hut was dark.

'Curfew ... Curfew. ...' And then turning his voice to Ngotho, 'And *you* again did nothing?'

Ngotho felt this like a pin pressed into his flesh. He was ready to accept everything, but not this.

'Listen, my son.'

But Boro had gone out. Ngotho had nobody to whom he could explain. For a long time they were not to see Boro's face.

Breaking the curfew order was not a very serious crime. It meant a fixed fine for everyone – young and old alike. But in this case, when the money for the fine had been taken, only Njeri was released. Kori would be sent to a detention camp, without trial. Ngotho's prophecy was materializing. But there in the homeguard post, the Chief was disappointed because the man he was really after had not been caught. But he did not lose hope.

One day Njoroge went to school early. He knew that something had happened to Ngotho who no longer looked anybody straight in the face; not even his wives. Njoroge was sure that if a child hit Ngotho, he would probably submit. He was no longer the man whose ability to keep home together had resounded from ridge to ridge. But Njoroge still believed in him and felt secure when Ngotho was near.

Ngotho's home now was a place where stories were no longer told, a place where no young men and women from the village gathered.

Through all this, Njoroge was still sustained by his love for and belief in education and his own role when the time came. And the difficulties of home seemed to have sharpened this appetite. Only education could make something out of this wreckage. He became more faithful to his studies. He would one day use all his learning to fight the white man, for he would continue the work that his father had started. When these moments caught him, he actually saw himself as a possible saviour of the whole God's country. Just let him get learning. Let that time come when he . . .

When Njoroge reached school, he found the other boys in a state of excitement. A small crowd of boys had gathered around the wall of the church. They were reading a letter to the headmaster, fixed to the wall. Every boy who came rushed there shouting and then would come out of the crowd quiet with a changed expression. Njoroge made his way through the crowd. He read the letter. His vision vanished at once. The fear that had caught the whole group attacked him too. For a time there was a tension in the atmosphere.

One boy said, 'They have done the same in Nyeri.'

'And Fort Hall.'

'Yes. I must not come back to this school.'

The headmaster came. He was shown the letter. At first he smiled carelessly and reassuringly to the boys. But as he read the letter his lips fell. Gingerly, he took out a razor and removed it, holding it only at the edges. His hands betrayed him.

'Has any of you touched it?'

'Nobody, sir,' the head boy said.

'Who came here the earliest?'

'It is I, sir.' A small boy came out from the crowd.

'Did you find the letter here?'

'I did not, sir. I did not look. It's Kamau who saw it.'

'Kamau, did you come after Njuguna?'

'Yes, sir. You see, sir, I was going to put my panga against the wall. Then I looked up. I saw the letter. At first I did not—'

'All right, Kamau. Njuguna, did you meet anybody on the way as you were coming to school?'

'No, sir.'

The question in the minds of most boys was: How had Kimathi come to their school? And that day there was an unusual air of gravity in the school.

In the evening, Njoroge related the whole incident to his mother.

'The letter said that the head of the headmaster plus the heads of forty children would be cut off if the school did not instantly close down. It was signed with Kimathi's name.'

'My son, you'll not go to that school any more. Education is not life.'

Njoroge felt a hurt comfort.

'I thought Mau Mau was on the side of the black people.'

'Sh! sh!' Nyokabi cautioned him. 'Don't you mention that tonight. Walls have ears.'

But Kamau told him a different thing.

'You'll be foolish to leave school. The letter may not be genuine. Besides do you really think you'll be safer at home? I tell you there's no safety anywhere. There's no hiding in this naked land.'

Njoroge did not leave school.

CHAPTER ELEVEN

Conditions went from bad to worse. No one could tell when he might be arrested for breaking the curfew. You could not even move across the courtyard at night. Fires were put out early for fear that any light would attract the attention of those who might be lurking outside. It was said that some European soldiers were catching people at night, and having taken them to the forest would release them and ask them to find their way back home. But when their backs were turned they would be shot dead in cold blood. The next day this would be announced as a victory over Mau Mau.

The boys too lived in fear. They did not know when the school would be attacked. Most of them had not heeded the warning of the letter. Like Njoroge they had continued going to school. Njoroge was now a big boy, almost a young man. The full force of the chaos that had come over the land was just beginning to be clear in his mind. All his brothers, except the lonely Kamau, were no longer at home. When the time for circumcision came, it was Kamau who met the cost. It was he who kept the home together, buying food, clothes and paying fees for Njoroge. But he rarely came to sleep at home.

Njoroge still had a father, a brother and two mothers, and so he clung to his vision of boyhood. With only a year to go before his examination for entrance to a secondary school, he worked hard at his books and his lessons.

Njoroge had not met Mwihaki since she went to the boarding school for girls. This was not an accident. Even before the emergency he had tried to avoid her. How could he have met her when her father and his were enemies in public? He almost felt the pain she must have felt when she had heard that her father had been attacked. Although Njoroge could not bring himself to condemn his father, yet he felt guilty and wished Mwihaki had been his own sister and not the daughter of Jacobo. Their last happy moment when they had stood holding hands before they went to hear all, still lingered in Njoroge's mind. It hurt him. Throughout the emergency, the fact that her father was a chief and a leader of the homeguards had made him feel even more acutely the need for a total separation. Yet at times he hungered for her company, for her delicate brown hands and clear innocent eyes.

One Saturday, Njoroge followed the long and broad road to the African shops where Kamau worked. Njoroge was lonely and wanted to find companionship. He always admired the big, strong muscles of Kamau as he held the saw, or the hammer, or the smoothing plane. He looked sure, as he hammered in a nail here and sawed a piece of wood there. . . . Njoroge often wondered whether he himself could ever have been like this. This time Njoroge found Kamau not working. There was an uneasy calm over the whole town.

'Is it well with you, brother?'

'It's just well! How is home?'

'Everything in good condition. Why are you all so grave?'

Kamau looked at Njoroge.

'Haven't you heard, that the barber and – and—? Six in all were taken from their houses three nights ago. They have been discovered dead in the forest.'

'Dead!'

'Yes!'

'The barber dead? But he cut my hair only – Oh, dead?'

'It's a sad business. You know them all. One was Nganga.'

'Nganga on whose land we have built?'

'Yes!'

Njoroge remembered that Nganga's wives had gone from one homeguard post to the next asking to be allowed to see their husband whom they said had been called from bed by a white man.

'Who killed them really, the white men?'

'Who can tell these days who kills who?'

'Nganga really dead!'

'Yes. And the barber.'

It was almost ridiculous to think that one would never see the six men again. Four of them had been some of the richest people and quite influential in all the land. Njoroge wondered if these were the Mau Mau. For only that could explain why the government people had slaughtered them in cold blood. Would his home be next? Boro was said to have gone to the forest. Njoroge shuddered to think about it.

Two days later. He was on his way home from the market place. He cut across the field as he did not want to follow the tarmac road. The deaths of the six men had created a kind of charged stillness in the village. Although there had been several deportations from the village and a few deaths, this was the first big direct blow by either Mau Mau or Serikali to the village community. Njoroge could now remember the carpenter whom at childhood he detested and who had befriended them at the hour of their trouble with stronger affection than he had ever felt when the carpenter was alive.

'Njoroge!' He did not hear it, and would have gone on except that now she was coming towards him. Mwihaki was tall, slim, with small pointed breasts. Her soft dark eyes looked burningly alive. The features of her face were now well-defined while her glossy mass of deep black hair had been dressed in a peculiar manner, alien to the village. This immediately reminded Njoroge of Lucia, Mwihaki's sister, who was now married with two children. He himself was tall with rather rough, hardened features, which made him look more of an adult than he actually was. He had always had about him a certain warm reserve that made him attractive and mysterious. At first he was shocked into a pleasant sensation and then later was embarrassed by the self-possession and assurance of this girl. How could she be Jacobo's daughter?

'I am sorry. I'd have passed you. You have changed much.'
That was how he rather hesitantly excused himself after the
usual greetings.

'Have I? You have changed too.' Her voice was still soft.
'Last week when I passed near your home I did not see you.'

Again he felt embarrassed. While he had for years been de-
liberately avoiding a meeting with her, she had at last taken the
initiative to seek him out.

'It's a long time since we last met,' he said.

'Yes. And much has happened in between – much more than
you and I could ever have dreamed of.'

'Much has happened ...' he echoed her words. Then he
asked, 'How's boarding school?'

'Nice. There you are in a kind of cloister.'

'And the country?'

'Bad. Like here.'

He thought he would change the subject.

'Well, I hope you'll enjoy your holidays,' he said, preparing
to go. 'I must go now. I must not delay you.' She did not
answer. Njoroge looked up at her.

'I'm so lonely here,' she at last said, with a frank, almost
childishly hurt voice. 'Everyone avoids me.'

His heart beat tom-tom. His sense of gallantry made him
say, 'Let's meet on Sunday.'

'Where?'

He paused to think of a suitable place.

'In the church.' That was where everyone went these
troubled days.

'No! Let's go there together. It would be like the old days.'

He did not resist the suggestion.

'All right. I shall be waiting for you near my home. When
you come, we shall go together. My home is on the way.'

'Go in peace.'

'Go in peace.'

Njoroge felt a small awareness stirring in him. And yet as he
went home he blamed himself for accepting this arrangement.

He almost turned round to call her back and cancel the whole thing.

He put on his best, a cheap nylon shirt and a well-pressed clean pair of khaki shorts. With khaki stockings and brown shoes made from the factory near his home town, he looked very smart. But now that he had slept off the excitement of meeting Mwihaki, he was afraid. He kept on saying 'I'm a fool, I am a fool.' But her voice, soft and clear, rang appealingly. *I am so lonely here.* Who could have thought of Mwihaki from her physical appearance as being lonely or troubled at heart? He prepared himself early and went to stroll on the path near his home. Then she came. Her white, low-necked blouse and pleated light brown skirt made him feel ashamed of his clothes. They moved on in silence. Only when she talked there was a little suppressed excitement in her voice.

It was a long time since she had met Njoroge. The memory of their hours together at school were still fresh in her mind. Mwihaki was not one to forget a small kindness, even if rendered so early in childhood. The dumb consolation this boy had tried to give her so early in her life had made an indelible impression on her. Again, Njoroge was different from the other boys. He had always held a fascination for her. He gave her peace and assurance. Much had happened between their two families. She knew that her father, at least, hated Ngotho. He did not care to hide the fact. His open hatred, she knew, had stemmed from Ngotho's public humiliation of Jacobo. Mwihaki could never tell the rights and wrongs of the affair. On the whole, she knew that her father must be right and Ngotho had behaved badly towards his benefactor. But she saw this only as a Jacobo–Ngotho affair that had nothing to do with her relationship with Njoroge. Her world and Njoroge's world stood somewhere outside petty prejudices, hatreds and class differences. She thought that Njoroge was of the same mind about these things and so had never come to realize that their many years of separation were not all that accidental. The declaration of emergency had not meant much to her. Yet as the years went and she heard stories of Mau Mau and how they could slash their opponents into pieces with Pangas, she became afraid. She had heard that Boro, Njoroge's brother, had gone into the forest, but she could not quite believe this. To her, the Mau Mau were people who did not belong to the village and certainly were not among the circle of her acquaintances.

The old preacher was in the pulpit. He spoke of the calamity that had befallen the Gikuyu people, a tribe that long ago walked with God, a tribe that had been chosen by God himself who had given it a beautiful land. Yet now blood flowed there freely, covering the land with deep, red sin. He talked of the young men and women who would never be seen any more. His face was dark as he talked of the many who were lying in the detention camps. Why was this so? It was because people had disobeyed the Creator, the Giver of Life. The children of Israel had refused to hearken unto the voice of Jehovah. They would be destroyed in the desert where they would be made to wander for forty years.

'Our people, what shall we do to escape the greater plague that is to come? We must turn to God. We must go on our knees and behold the animal hung on the tree yonder. Then all our wounds will heal at once. We shall be washed by the blood of the Lamb. Our people, what is said in the Holy Scriptures is what I will tell you now. . . .

'Let's pray. . . .'

They all knelt down and prayed for the land. Some cried – crying for those whom they would see no more.

A short man went into the pulpit. Njoroge looked at him closely. His face seemed familiar. The man began to speak. And then Njoroge remembered. This was the worldly teacher they used to call *Uuu*. His moustache was not there. Teacher Isaka had gone to Nyeri the year Njoroge finished the first school. Since then, Njoroge had not heard of him. Isaka now looked distinctly holy. This was what it meant to be a Revivalist.

'Turn to the Gospel according to St Matthew, Chapter 24, and beginning to read from line 4.'

There was a shuffle of leaves.

'Let's begin to read. . . .'

'And Jesus answered and said unto them: Take heed that no man deceive you.

'For many shall come in My name, saying, I am Christ; and shall deceive many.

'And ye shall hear of wars and rumours of wars: see that ye be not troubled: for all these things must come to pass, but the end is not yet.

'For nation shall rise against nation, and kingdom against kingdom: and there shall be famines, and pestilences, and earthquakes, in divers places.

'All these are the beginning of sorrows.

Then shall they deliver you up to be afflicted, and shall kill you: and ye shall be hated of all nations for My name's sake.

'And then shall many be offended, and shall betray one another, and shall hate one another.

'And many false prophets shall rise, and shall deceive many.

'And because iniquity shall abound, the love of many shall wax cold.

'*But he that shall endure unto the end, the same shall be saved. . . .*'

He read on. But when he came to verse 33, he stopped and stared at all the people in the church. Then he raised his voice and went on:

'Verily I say unto you, This generation shall not pass till all these things be fulfilled. . . .'

It was as if darkness too had fallen into the building and there was no one to light the way.

They went along in silence. It was late in the day for the service had taken many hours. It was Mwihaki who quickly whispered, 'Let's follow the old path.'

Njoroge agreed. The old path was the one they used to follow on their way from school.

'Do you think what he said was true?'

'What? He said many things.'

'That Jesus will come soon?'

Njoroge started. He too was thinking about what their old teacher predicted about the world. He had been impressed because it all looked so true. War, diseases, pestilence, insecurity, betrayal, family disintegrations – Njoroge had seen all these. Oh, yes, he was inclined to agree with the teacher. But he did not like the teacher's voice as he cried, hysterically, 'Repent you know. For the Kingdom of God is near.'

Had the country really been reduced to this? Would the Second Coming see to the destruction of all life in this world?'

'I don't know,' he at last said.

'Dear Jesus,' she murmured to herself.

They came near her home. She said, 'Let's go in.'

Njoroge protested. Her face darkened. Quietly, almost inaudibly, she said, 'I know. It's because father is a chief.'

'Please—' He knew he was beaten. She had seen into his heart. They went in. Jacobo's home was not as awesome as it used to be. Long ago when Njoroge and the other children of the ridge used to work for Jacobo picking pyrethrum flowers he had always felt a weight in his stomach whenever he came near this house. He did not like looking at it for a long time because he had always feared that Jacobo or Juliana might come out only to see him staring at their European household. But even now the whole place was quite impressive. Njoroge hoped that Jacobo would not be there. The Chief was rarely seen. And when someone saw him approach his home, he automatically knew that something was wrong. The name of the Chief was becoming a terror in the land. Njoroge could remember how he once saw three women dash into a bush as they were coming from the market. Njoroge had wondered why. But on looking in front he saw the Chief. He too had feared, but it had been too late for him to disappear.

When Mwihaki went into the kitchen he stood up and looked at the photographs that were hung all around the room. There was Lucia as a child, as a teacher, and two taken at her wedding. There was her brother, John, who had gone overseas. Where was Mwihaki? He longed to see how she looked in a photograph. Then there was a sound of feet at the door. Njoroge turned. Jacobo, his wife, Juliana, and three homeguards with rifles were entering the house. Njoroge, still looking at them, went to his chair and sat on the edge with his left hand on the seat while with his right hand he played with a button.

'How's school?' Jacobo asked, after he and his homeguards had found seats. Juliana had gone to the kitchen. Jacobo looked tired. He was not the proud farmer of old.

' 'Tis all right.'

'In which class are you now?'

'Standard VIII. I'm doing K.A.P.E. this year.'

'Then you'll go to High School?'

'Yes, if I pass.'

Now Njoroge felt a little brave and sat on the chair squarely. Jacobo's face was a little wrinkled. There was a change in his voice as he said,

'I hope you do well. It is such as you who must work hard and rebuild the country.'

Njoroge felt something jump in him. He saw himself rebuilding the whole country. For a moment he glowed with that possibility. . . .

He stole a glance at the homeguards. He found them looking at him. Their red jerseys reminded him of the dead barber.

They went to a hill. It was near their home. She lay on the grass on her left side and faced him. He sat upright and looked at the plain below. The plain was usually full of water, especially during the rainy season. Now it was dry. Mwihaki played with the button on his back pocket. Then she sat upright and too looked at the plain.

She said, 'I was afraid.'

'You should not be afraid,' Njoroge said.

'But I was— When the teacher said the world would soon come to an end.'

Njoroge turned to her and looked at her for a moment. He tried to smile indulgently but he failed. His face remained contracted into small creases as if he were recalling something.

'It is very hard to imagine everything destroyed – I mean flattened out into a plain like this one. You imagine the blood and the bones of all people, white and black, mine and yours, all. . . .'

'Stop!' She shut her eyes as if she did not want to see the sight of a lake of blood and a plain of bones.

'I see you are afraid,' he said, again trying to smile indulgently. He truly felt brave because she was afraid, and she was only a woman, a girl.

'You see,' she said when she had recovered. 'It frightened me to think that I may go to bed one night and wake up to find everything gone – all destroyed.'

'But you would be destroyed too, so you won't see anything.'

'Don't laugh.'

'I am not laughing.'

This was true for he too was thinking of the possibility of what she had said. What if all people were destroyed and he alone was left? What could he do with his learning which he had hoped to use in rescuing the country from ruin? Then he thought: What if it was only his family which would be destroyed? He shivered in the stomach. He quickly asked, 'When are you going back?'

'Next week.'

'So soon?' She didn't hear.

'Njoroge, do you think all this was actually prophesied by Isaiah and all the other prophets?'

'It is in the Bible.'

'Because I was thinking that if Jesus knew, really knew,

about this thing in our country, He could have stopped it. Don't you think so?'

Njoroge believed in the righteousness of God. Therefore he thought all this would work out well in the end. And he felt a bit awed to imagine that God may have chosen him to be the instrument of His Divine Service. So he just said, 'God works in a mysterious way.'

'You know what really worries me is this. It is my father. He used to be so kind and gentle, especially with me. He annoyed me sometimes of course but that was nothing. He always came to my side when mother scolded me. I enjoyed his smile and thought I would like a husband with teeth like his. ...' She stopped, and thought for a moment. Then she looked down as if she was puzzled by something. 'But now he is uncommunicative. The gun and the pistol he carries make him a stranger to me. Oh, if only I was bigger and really strong, I would do something. ... Perhaps you don't believe it, but—'

'It is the same everywhere,' he said irrelevantly. All things would change. Only people had to believe in and trust God. She went on, not seeing that he was not really attending.

'I hate to think that he may have killed some man because at night he wakes and says that he heard some people talking of his own death. And people you know are always avoiding me, even girls of my age. It is, oh—'

She burst into tears. Njoroge was horrified to see the tears of a big girl. All girls were like this, he thought. Yet he would not have believed this of Mwihaki. He pulled a blade of grass and chewed it. And Mwihaki took her handkerchief and wiped her eyes. Njoroge looked away. The plain below was quiet and big. For a time Njoroge forgot Mwihaki; he was lost in speculations about his vital role in the country. He remembered David rescuing a whole country from the curse of Goliath.

'You must think me a silly weak girl, but you know I think the people have sinned.'

He felt as he had felt when the old preacher talked about Sin. If Gikuyu people had sinned, then he might be sent to them by

94

God. He remembered Samuel and many other prophets. But he said, 'Is it possible for a whole nation to sin?'

'One man sins, God punishes all.'

He thought: She is right. God had done this often to the children of Israel. But He always sent somebody to rescue them.

'. . . and the sin could be committed by anyone, you or I . . .'

He was startled out of this vision. He had at times felt like this. For instance, that day his mother quarrelled with his father. He had felt guilty as if he had been responsible. He suppressed this and looking at Mwihaki said firmly, 'Peace shall come to this land!' His task of comforting people had begun.

'Oh, Njoroge, do you really think so?' She said, creeping near him as if he was the comfort himself.

'Yes. Sunshine always follows a dark night. We sleep knowing and trusting that the sun will rise tomorrow.' He liked this piece of reasoning. But he was rather annoyed when she laughingly said, 'Tomorrow. Tomorrow never comes. I would rather think of today.' But her eyes dilated like a child's as she looked hopefully at him. An idea came to her. She held Njoroge by the neck and shook him excitedly.

'What is it?' asked Njoroge, startled.

'Something. Suppose you and I go from here so that we come back when the dark night is over. . . .'

'But—'

'I could be such a nice sister to you and I could cook you very tasty food and—'

'Just a minute.'

'It is a good idea, isn't it?'

Njoroge was very serious. He saw his vision wrecked by such a plan. And what would God think if he deserted his mission like this?

'No. No. How can we leave our parents alone?'

'We could—'

'And tell me where would we go and what could we eat?'

She looked disappointed, but she easily laughed it off. She said, 'Don't be so serious. I was only joking.'

Njoroge was puzzled and felt slight irritation against this girl. He could never understand her. But he too tried to laugh and said, 'Of course I knew.'

She thought that he was annoyed and soothed him.

'But we shall remain friends and always trust each other.'

'We *are* friends,' he said.

'But you never come to see me when—'

He became at once aware of the difference between them.

'We don't see each other.'

'When I come back, you will not let me alone?' she appealed, again her eyes dilating. She was sitting close to him. She touched the collar of his shirt and then rubbed off an insect that was walking along it. He looked at her in a brotherly fashion. He had now quickly forgotten their differences. To him she was a girl who might have easily been his sister.

He said, 'When you come back, I shall be with you.'

'It is a promise?'

'Of course.'

They moved together, so as not be be caught by the darkness. A bird cried. And then another. And these two, a boy and a girl went forward each lost in their own world, for a time oblivious of the bigger darkness over the whole land.

CHAPTER TWELVE

Mr Howlands felt a certain gratifying pleasure. The machine he had set in motion was working. The blacks were destroying the blacks. They would destroy themselves to the end. What did it matter with him if the blacks in the forest destroyed a whole village? What indeed did it matter except for the fact that labour would diminish? Let them destroy themselves. Let them fight against each other. The few who remained would be satisfied with the land the white man had preserved for them. Yes, Mr Howlands was coming to enjoy his work. At the beginning of the emergency, when he had been called from the farm, he had been angry. He had at times longed to go back to the life of a farmer. But as the years went, the assertive desire to reduce to obedience had conquered, enabling him to do his work with a thoroughness that would not have been possible with many of his age. He looked up at Chief Jacobo. A wicked smile lit his face. The desire to kick the Chief was uppermost in his mind. The Chief was grinning.

'Are you sure it's Boro who is leading the gang?'

'Well, one can't be quite sure, but—'

'What?'

'This man, as you are aware, is known to be dangerous. I told you so when you and I talked together before he ran away. Well, I think, I mean there are rumours that he probably comes home ... but even if this is not the case, Ngotho surely knows his son's hiding-place.'

'Haven't you planted men to watch Ngotho's movements and report on them?'

Mr Howlands always felt that soon he would come to grips with Ngotho. Ngotho was his foe. But Mr Howlands could not explain to himself why he always waived plans to bring Ngotho to a submissive humiliation. Yet this was what he wanted. This would be the crowning glory of his career before his triumphal return to farming life. Meanwhile he would resist all Jacobo's moves to have Ngotho arrested just now. He had often resisted this just as much as he had resisted his wife's requests that she and Stephen should go back to England for this time being. Stephen was now in the High School for Europeans which was a few miles from Siriana.

Jacobo was long in answering.

'I have, sir, but there's something else. I didn't, you know, want to tell you, but a few days ago I received this note in an envelope dropped at my door.' The Chief fumbled in the inner pockets of his coat and took out a hand-written note which he handed to the curious Howlands.

STOP YOUR MURDEROUS ACTIVITIES. OR ELSE WE SHALL COME FOR YOUR HEAD. THIS IS OUR LAST WARNING.

'Why! Have you received more?'

'Yes – two. But—'

'What did you do with them, you fool?' Mr Howlands was furious. He stood up. Jacobo moved a few steps back to the door. Howlands could never understand such ignorance. To receive two notes of warning and keep quiet! After a time he cooled down.

'All right, leave this one with me. Where do you think they come from?'

'From Ngotho.'

'How do you know?'

'Who else could easily come to my house? A few months ago, his youngest son was at my house—'

'Doing what?'

'Well, he's really a schoolboy, and, he had, eh, I mean, my daughter—'

Mr Howlands could not understand all this. Jacobo must be mad.

'All right. Leave this with me. You can have more home-

98

guards if you want. You must not leave your house without a
guard. Watch Ngotho's every step.'

'Yes, sir.'

'And by the way, when the new homeguard post is ready,
you and your family better move there.'

'Yes, sir.'

It was a hot January morning. Two young men walked along
a narrow cattle path, carelessly clutching their Bibles and hymn
books. Behind them were a group of men and women, also
holding Bibles and hymn books. They were discussing the
saving power of Christ. Farther behind still were women gaily
dressed in Sunday best. They were joyously singing.

Nitugu-u-kugoca Je-e-Jesu
Jesu Ga-a-tuurume Ka Ngai,
Jesu, Thakame yaku iithera-agia mehia
Ndakugo-o-ca Mwathani.

We praise you Jesus
Jesus the Lamb of God.
Jesus Thy blood cleans away my sins
I praise you O Lord.

All of them were going to a Christian gathering a few miles
away from the town.

'Are we nearly there?' Njoroge asked the other young man.
His name was Mucatha.

'No. We have not yet come to the wood I told you about.'

'It is far, then.'

'Not very far. I've been there on foot many times.'

'Will there be many people?'

'Yes. Many women.'

'Why women?'

'Where are the men?'

'Why, we?'

'Two only.'

'There are others.'

'Maybe.'

They both laughed and quickly fell silent. Njoroge thought how wonderful it would all have been if Mwihaki had been with them. But on this vacation she had not come home. She had gone to stay with Lucia. Njoroge always enjoyed reading her letters. During the second term holidays they had met quite often. Only he never repeated the visit to her home. They had found a number of things to talk about. He could still remember her words which had always encouraged him when confronted with a difficulty. 'Njoroge, I know you'll do well.' He had gone to the exam room with them. He would always be grateful to his mother, who had first sent him to school, and to Mwihaki. Yet what if he failed? That would be the end of all. What was a future without education? However, he trusted to God to carry him through.

'There now! This is the wood.'

'Oh! It's so thick, it frightens me.'

They stood on a rock.

'Do you see over there?'

'Beyond the dark wood?'

'Yes. Beyond, to the left of that hill.'

Njoroge could see a small hill in the distance.

'I see.'

'That's where the meeting is going to be.'

They moved down. Teacher Isaka and the others were nearer. They were still absorbed in their talk of salvation. The cattle path widened and wound through the dense wood. Suddenly, Njoroge heard a voice.

'Stop!'

Both stopped. Fright gripped them. For there, standing in front of them, was a white military officer.

'Mikono juu.'

They put up their hands so that their Bibles and hymn books were in the air as if they were displaying the word of God for all to see.

100

'Kuja hapa.'

They went nearer. A pistol was pointed at them. Soon the group of men who had been behind came. They went through the same process and lined up behind Njoroge and Mucatha. The women came, saw the scene, and the singing died with their steps. The women were first interrogated. They were then allowed to continue their journey. It was then that Njoroge looked around and saw that they were surrounded by many soldiers who lay hidden in the bush, with machine-guns menacingly pointed to the road. Njoroge clutched the Bible more firmly.

They were all made to squat and produce their documents. Fortunately Njoroge and Mucatha had letters from the former headmaster which indicated that they were schoolboys. The men at the back were not so lucky. One of them was beaten so much that he urinated on his legs. But he did not plead for mercy. The only thing he constantly said was 'Jesus'.

Isaka squatted and calmly watched the scene. He had no documents. When the white soldier shouted at him, Isaka answered in a calm, almost resigned tone. Where had he left the documents? Satan had made him forget them at home. But the white soldier knew better. Isaka was a Mau Mau. Again Isaka replied that Jesus had saved him and he could not exchange Jesus with Mau Mau. The officer looked at him with reddening eyes. Yet he did not touch him. Njoroge wondered if he was afraid of Isaka. There was something strange in the teacher's calm. When the others were allowed to go Isaka was made to remain. He did not protest.

'Come this way and we'll see what Jesus will do for you.'

He was led into the thick dark wood. Before the others had gone very far, they heard one horrible scream that rang across the forest. They dared not turn their heads. Njoroge tried to hold his breath so that his stomach was taut. They went a few more steps. Suddenly there was one other scream which was swallowed by a deafening report of machine-guns. Then silence.

'They have killed him,' one of the men said some time after the report. Njoroge suddenly felt sick, sick of everything. It was to him painfully unbelievable that he would see Isaka, the worldly teacher they used to call *Uuu*, no more.

'Don't you believe in anything?'

'No. Nothing. Except revenge.'

'Return of the lands?'

'The lost land will come back to us maybe. But I've lost too many of those whom I loved for land to mean much to me. It would be a cheap victory.' Boro was a bit more communicative as he sat with his lieutenant on a look-out a few miles from their new hide-out. The old hide-out had been in the wood where Isaka had been summarily executed into nothing. The patrol had been after the group that was led by Boro.

Boro had now been in the forest for a considerable time. His own dare-devil action, for he did not care what happened to him personally, had made him a leader of the other Freedom Fighters. The ripe hour of his youth had been spent in bloodshed in the big war. This was the only thing he could do efficiently.

Boro had always told himself that the real reason for his flight to the forest was a desire to fight for freedom. But this fervour had soon worn off. His mission became a mission of revenge. This was the only thing that could now give him fire and boldness. If he killed a single white man, he was exacting a vengeance for a brother killed.

'And Freedom?' the lieutenant continued.

'An illusion. What Freedom is there for you and me?'

'Why then do we fight?'

'To kill. Unless you kill, you'll be killed. So you go on killing and destroying. It's a law of nature. The white man too fights and kills with gas, bombs, and everything.'

'But don't you think there's something wrong in fighting and killing unless you're doing so for a great cause like ours?'

'What great cause is ours?'

'Why, Freedom and the return of our lost heritage.'

'Maybe there's something in that. But for me Freedom is meaningless unless it can bring back a brother I lost. Because it can't do that, the only thing left to me is to fight, to kill and rejoice at any who falls under my sword. But enough. Chief Jacobo must die.'

'Yes. You have said this many times.'

'I have said so many times,' Boro repeated quietly.

'And you delay.'

'I wonder why I delay. You know sometimes you feel something here. But it cannot be helped. He has not heeded any one of the warnings we've sent him. Look at the way he treated many of the squatters who were sent away from the Rift Valley.'

'Yes.'

'And with him, Howlands.'

'He is a dangerous man.'

'Jacobo must be shot alone. We don't want more deaths just now.'

The lieutenant could never understand Boro. At one breath he would talk of killing and killing as the law of the land and then in the next breath would caution care.

'Who's going to do it?'

'I will.'

'No! We cannot let you go. We cannot do without you.'

If I'm caught, you'll take over. I've shown you everything.'

'No, no! One of us will—'

'This is my personal affair.'

'But I think we should cast lots.'

'We shall see.'

They went back to their hide-out.

CHAPTER THIRTEEN

'Njoroge is going to High School.'

'High School!'

'Yes. He has gone through K.A.P.E.'

Ngotho was pleased. And Nyokabi and Njeri were full of joy at the news. For the first time for many years something like a glimmer of light shone in Ngotho's eyes. He could even be seen making an effort to walk upright. Here at last was a son who might be a credit to the family. Here was a son who might eventually be a match for the Howlands and the Jacobos and any others who at all despised him. Kamau too was pleased. He hoped he could go on helping Njoroge. Njoroge might do something for the family.

Njoroge was happy. His first impulse when he learnt that he had gone through was to kneel down and thank God for all He had done for him. 'Give me more and more learning and make me the instrument of Thy light and peace.' To go to Secondary School, the big mission school at Siriana, was no small achievement.

He was to learn later that he had been the only boy in all that area who would go to High School. Mwihaki too had passed. But because she had not done very well, she would only be going to a teacher training school a few miles from her boarding school. Njoroge was at first overjoyed to see he had beaten the daughter of Jacobo, but then felt sorry that she had not been able to continue.

The news of his success passed from hill to hill. In spite of the troubled time, people still retained a genuine interest in education. Whatever their differences, interest in knowledge and book-learning was the one meeting point between people such as Boro, Jacobo and Ngotho. Somehow the Gikuyu people always saw their deliverance as embodied in education. When the time for Njoroge to leave came near, many people contributed money so that he could go. He was no longer the son of Ngotho but the son of the land.

On the last Sunday he met Mwihaki. They went to the same hill. Njoroge had now a new feeling of pride and power for at last his way seemed clear. The land needed him and God had given him an opening so that he might come back and save his family and the whole country. It was a year now since he and Mwihaki had been to the same hill. Mwihaki had not changed much. She now ate blade after blade of grass. She did not sit so very close to him as she had done the first time. They talked about many things, but nothing was said about the one thing that was foremost in their own hearts.

Then she asked him, 'When will you go?'

'Early next month.'

'Siriana is a good school.'

'Oh, yes!'

'When people go away, they tend to forget those that they leave behind.'

'Do they?'

She was hurt. But she said, 'Yes. What will you do after all your learning? I am sure you will be a big man.'

'As a matter of fact, I have not thought out my plans. But I would probably like to go to Makerere or Britain like your brother.'

'My brother went to America, not Britain.'

'Well, it doesn't matter,' he said, moving close to her as if he was aware of her presence for the first time. She was looking at the ground where she was trying to draw something on a mould of soil – mole's soil. He wondered why she was not looking at him. Could she be feeling jealous?

'And after that?'

He became serious and a little distant. He was again in his vision.

'Our country has great need of us.'

'Do you think the country really needs you?'

'Yes,' he said rather irritably. Was she doubting him? 'The country needs me. It needs you. And the remnant. We must get together and rebuild the country. That was what your father told me the day that I was at your home.'

'The country is so dark now,' she whispered to herself.

'The sun will rise tomorrow,' he said triumphantly, looking at her as if he would tell her that he would never lose faith, knowing as he did that God had a secret plan.

'You are always talking about tomorrow, tomorrow. You are always talking about *the* country and *the* people. What is tomorrow? And what is *the People* and *the Country* to you?' She had suddenly stopped what she had been doing and was looking at him with blazing eyes. Njoroge saw this and was afraid. He did not want to make her angry. He was pained. He looked at her and then at the plain, the country beyond stretching on, on to the distant hills shrouded in the mist.

'Don't be angry, Mwihaki. For what can I say now? You and I can only put faith in hope. Just stop for a moment, Mwihaki, and imagine. If you knew that all your days life will always be like this with blood flowing daily and men dying in the forest, while others daily cry for mercy; if you knew even for one moment that this would go on for ever, then life would be meaningless unless bloodshed and death were a meaning. Surely this darkness and terror will not go on for ever. Surely there will be a sunny day, a warm sweet day after all this tribulation, when we can breathe the warmth and purity of God. . . .'

She lay quietly now with her head near him. Her eyes dilated with a pleasure which was warm to her. She wanted to hear the boy go on talking, preaching hope. She could now trust him. She could see the sunny day tomorrow and this could make her forget the present troubles. If every man came to breathe the warmth and the purity of God, then hatred, and—

'Are you sleeping?'

'No! no!' she said quickly.

'The sun goes down. We should go home.'

They rose to go. When parting she looked at him and firmly said, 'You will do well.'

Njoroge felt a low in his heart and for a time was ashamed of having thought Mwihaki jealous. He said, 'Thank you, Mwihaki. You have been like a true sister to me.'

She whispered 'Thank you'. She watched him go and then turned away her head. She took out her handkerchief and rubbed something wet on her cheeks while she ran towards her home faster, and faster.

CHAPTER FOURTEEN

Siriana Secondary School was a well-known centre of learning. Being one of the earliest schools to be started in the colony, it had expanded much due mainly to the efforts of its missionary founders.

To Njoroge, coming here was nearly the realization of his dreams. He would for the first time be taught by white men. And this was what confused him. Though he had never come into real contact with white men, yet if one had met him and had abused him or tried to put him in his place, Njoroge would have understood. He would have even known how to react. But not when he met some who could smile and laugh. Not when he met some who made friends with him and tried to help him in his Christian progress.

Here again, he met boys from many tribes. Again if these had met him and had tried to practise dangerous witchcraft on him, he would have understood. But instead he met boys who were like him in every way. He made friends and worked with Nandi, Luo, Wakamba, and Giriama. They were boys who had hopes and fears, loves and hatreds. If he quarrelled with any or if he hated any, he did so as he would have done with any other boy from his village.

The school itself was an adobe of peace in a turbulent country. Here it was possible to meet with God, not only in the cool shelter of the chapel, where he spent many hours, but also in the quietness of the library. For the first time he felt he would escape the watchful eyes of misery and hardship that had for a long time stared at him in his home. Here he would organize his thoughts and make definite plans for the future. He was sure that with patience and hard work, his desire to have learning would be fulfilled. Maybe the sun would soon rise to announce a new day.

Siriana Secondary School took part in inter-schools sports meetings at which some Asian and European schools took part. The Hill School was a famous school for European boys.

The Hill School sent a team of boys to Siriana for football. It was four o'clock. Along with the eleven players were some who were mere spectators. Njoroge did not play football and it happened that he fell into conversation with one of the visitors not actively engaged in playing. But as soon as Njoroge spoke to the boy, he felt that he must have seen him somewhere else. The boy was tall, with long brown hair that kept on being blown on to his face by the wind. He had to keep on swinging his head to make the threads of hair return to their proper places.

'I think I've seen you before,' Njoroge at last said as he took the boy round.

'Have you?' The boy looked up at Njoroge full in the eyes. At first he seemed puzzled. Then his face brightened up. He said 'Oh, do you come from Kipanga?'

'Yes. That's where I've seen you before.'

'I remember. You are the son of Ngotho who—' The boy suddenly stopped.

'My name is Stephen. Stephen Howlands.'

'I am Njoroge.'

They walked on in silence. Njoroge saw he was not afraid of Stephen. Here in school, Stephen was a boy. Njoroge could not be afraid of a boy.

'When did you come here?'

'At the beginning of this year. And you?'

'Been in Hill School for two years.'

'Which school did you go to before you came here?'

'Nairobi. What about you?'

'I went to Kamahou Intermediate School.'

'Is that the school you went to when you passed near our home?'

'No. That one was Kamae Primary School and went up to Standard IV. Did you see me?'

'Yes.' Stephen could easily recall the many times he had hidden in the hedge near his home with the object of speaking to Njoroge or any other of the children. Yet whenever they came near he felt afraid.

'We didn't see you.'

'I used to hide near the road. I wanted to speak with some of you.' Stephen was losing his shyness.

'Why didn't you?'

'I was afraid.'

'Afraid?'

'Yes. I was afraid that you might not speak to me or you might not need my company.'

'Was it all that bad?'

'Not so much.' He did not want sympathy.

'I am sorry I ran away from you. I too was afraid.'

'Afraid?' It was Stephen's turn to wonder.

'Yes. I too was afraid of you.'

'But I meant no harm?'

'All the same I was. How could I tell what you meant to do?'

'Strange.'

'Yes. It's strange. It's strange how you do fear something because your heart is already prepared to fear because maybe you were brought up to fear that something, or simply because you found others fearing. ... That's how it's with me. When my brothers went to Nairobi and walked in the streets, they came home and said that they didn't like the way Europeans looked at them.

'I suppose it's the same everywhere. I have heard many friends say they didn't like the way Africans looked at them. And when you are walking in Nairobi or in the country, though the sky may be clear and the sun is smiling, you are still

110

not free to enjoy the friendliness of the sky because you are aware of an electric tension in the air. . . . You cannot touch it, you cannot see it . . . but you are aware of it all the time.'

'Yes. Till sometimes it can be maddening. You are afraid of it and if you try to run away from it, you know it's all futile because wherever you go it's there before you.'

'It's bad.'

'It's bad,' agreed Njoroge. They felt close together, united by a common experience of insecurity and fear no one could escape.

'Yes the country is so cool and so absorbing. . . .'

'It's a land of sunshine and rain and wind, mountains and valleys and plains. Oh – but the sunshine—'

'But so dark now.'

'Yes – so dark, but things will be all right.'

Njoroge still believed in the future. Hope of a better day was the only comfort he could give to a weeping child. He did not know that this faith in the future could be a form of escape from the reality of the present.

The two had moved away from the crowd and were standing together under a black wattle tree.

'I'll be away from home soon.'

'Where will you go?'

'To England.'

'But that's your home?'

'No. It isn't. I was born here and I have never been to England. I don't even want to go there.'

'Do you have to go?'

'Yes. Father did not want to, but my mother wanted us to go.'

'When will you go?'

'Next month.'

'I hope you'll come back?'

A wave of pity for this young man who had to do what he did not want to do filled Njoroge. At least, he, Njoroge, would rise and fall with his country. He had nowhere else to go.

'I want to come back.'

'Is your father going with you?'

'No. He'll remain here. But – but – you sometimes get a feeling that you're going away from someone for ever. ... That's how I feel and that's what makes it all so awful.'

Again silence settled between them. Njoroge wanted to change the subject.

'They have changed sides.'

'Let's go and cheer.'

The two moved back to the field, again shy with each other. They moved into two different directions as if they were afraid of another contact.

Mwihaki wrote frequently. Njoroge could remember her first letter just before she went to the Teacher Training School.

Dear Njoroge,

You don't know how much I miss you. For the last few days I have been thinking of nothing but you. The knowledge that you're so far from me makes the thoughts very painful. But I know what you are doing there. I know you'll do well because you've got determination. I trust you.

I am going to the Training School next week. Living here has been hell for me. Father has changed much. He seems to be fearing something. Every day there have been some new arrests and some houses burnt down by Mau Mau. Yesterday I found some people being beaten and they were crying, oh so horribly, begging for mercy. I don't know what's happening. Fear in the air. Not a fear of death – it's a fear of living.

I am caught in it and if this goes on I feel as if I could go mad ... I'm telling all this to show you how glad I am at the prospects of escaping away from it all ...

Njoroge wondered what changes he would find at home

112

when the end of the year came. Did he really want to go home? If he went misery would gnaw at his peace of mind. He did not want to go back. He thought it would be a more worthwhile homecoming if he stayed here till he had equipped himself with learning.

CHAPTER FIFTEEN

It was a cold Monday morning. Njoroge had gone through the first two terms and now was in his third. It would soon end. Njoroge woke up as usual, said his prayers and prepared himself for the morning parade. It was such a pleasant morning in spite of the cold. After the roll call he went to the chapel for a communion with God, and then to the dining hall for breakfast; that was always the daily routine. He ate his breakfast quickly for he had not yet finished the preparation for the previous night.

The first class was English. Njoroge loved English literature.

'Why, you look happy today,' a boy teased him.

'But I'm always happy,' he said.

'Not when we're doing maths,' another boy put in.

They laughed. Njoroge's laughter rang in the class. The first boy who had spoken said, 'See, see how he's laughing. He is happy because this is an English class.'

'Do you want me to cry?' Njoroge asked. He felt buoyant.

'No. It's only that my mother tells me that a man should not be too happy in the morning. It's an ill-omen.'

'Don't be superstitious.'

Yet Njoroge did not like the last observation. All through the week that had passed, he had been assailed by bad dreams. The dreams had affected him so much that he had been unable to write to Mwihaki. Tonight, however, he would write to her. He wanted to tell her that Stephen had gone back to England and his sister had accompanied them. She would however come back to continue her missionary work. When he first met Stephen he had written to her, telling her about his own impression of Stephen. 'He looked lonely and sad' he had finished.

There was a lot of shouting in the room. Then one boy whispered: 'Teacher. Hush!' There was silence in the room. The teacher came in. He was always on time. Njoroge was often surprised by these missionaries' apparent devotion to their work. One might have thought that teaching was to them life and death. Yet they were white men. They never talked of colour; they never talked down to Africans; and they could work closely, joke, and laugh with their black colleagues who came from different tribes. Njoroge at times wished the whole country was like this. This seemed a little paradise, a paradise where children from all walks of life and of different religious faiths could work together without any consciousness. Many people believed the harmony in the school came because the headmaster was a strange man who was severe with everyone, black and white alike. If he was quick to praise what was good, he was equally quick to suppress what he thought was evil. He tried to bring out the good qualities in all, making them work for the good name of the school. But he believed that the best, the really excellent could only come from the white man. He brought up his boys to copy and cherish the white man's civilization as the only hope of mankind and especially of the black races. He was automatically against all black politicians who in any way made people to be discontented with the white man's rule and civilizing mission.

Njoroge was in the middle of answering a question when the headmaster came to the door. The teacher went out to see what the headmaster wanted. When he came back, he looked at Njoroge and told him that he was wanted outside.

His heart beat hard. He did not know what the headmaster could have to say to him. A black car stood outside the office. But it was only when Njoroge entered the office and saw two police officers that he knew that the car outside had something to do with him. Njoroge's heart pounded with fear.

The headmaster said something to the two officers who immediately withdrew.

115

'Sit down, my boy.' Njoroge, whose knees had already failed him, gladly sank into the chair. The headmaster looked at him with compassionate eyes. He continued, 'I'm sorry to hear this about your family.'

Njoroge watched the missionary's face and lips. His own face did not change but Njoroge listened keenly with clenched teeth.

'You're wanted at home. It's a sad business ... but whatever your family may have made you do or take in the past, remember Christ is there at the door, knocking, waiting to be admitted. That's the path we've tried to make you follow. We hope you'll not disappoint us.' The headmaster sounded as if he would cry.

But when Njoroge went to the car he realized that the headmaster had not given him a clue as to what his family had done. His words of comfort had only served to increase Njoroge's torment.

He would never forget his experience in the post. That particular homeguard post was popularly known as the House of Pain. The day following his arrival in the post he was called into a small room. Two European officers were present. One had a red beard.

'What's your name?' the red beard asked, while the grey eyes looked at him ferociously.

'Njo-ro-ge.'

'How old are you?'

'I think 19 or thereabouts.'

'Sema affande!' one of the homeguards outside the small room shouted.

'Affande.'

'Have you taken the Oath?'

'No!'

'Sema affende!' barked the same homeguard.

'No. Affendi.'

'How many have you taken?'

'I said none affendi!'

The blow was swift. It blinded him so that he saw darkness. He had not see the grey eyes rise.

'Have you taken Oath?'

'I-am-a-school-boy-affendi,' he said, automatically lifting his hands to his face.

'How many Oaths have you taken?'

'None, sir.'

Another blow. Tears rolled down his cheeks in spite of himself. He remembered the serenity of his school. It was a lost paradise.

'Do you know Boro?'

'He's my – brother—'

'Where is he?'

'I – don't – know—'

Njoroge lay on the dusty floor. The face of the grey eyes had turned red. He never once spoke except to call him Bloody Mau Mau. A few seconds later Njoroge was taken out by the two homeguards at the door. He was senseless. He was covered with blood where the hob-nailed shoes of the grey eyes had done their work.

He woke up from the coma late in the night. He heard a woman screaming in a hut not far from the one in which he lay. Could it be Njeri? Or Nyokabi? He shuddered to think about it. He longed to see them all once again before he died. For he thought this was the end. Perhaps death was not bad at all. It sent you into a big sleep from which you never awoke to the living fears, the dying hopes, the lost visions.

They had not finished with him. He was in the room the next day. What would he do if they asked him the same questions again? Tell a lie? Would they leave him alone if he said yes to every question? He doubted it. His body had swollen all over. But the worst thing for him was the fact he was still in the dark about all this affair.

'You are Njoroge?'

'Yees.'

'Have you taken Oath?' All eyes turned to him. Njoroge

hesitated for a moment. He noticed that Mr Howlands was also present. The grey eyes took the momentary hesitation and said, 'Mark, you tell us the truth. If you tell the truth, we shall let you go.' The pain in his body came and asked him to say *Yes*. But he instinctively said *No* withdrawing a few steps to the door. Nobody touched him.

'Who murdered Jacobo?' Mr Howlands asked for the first time. For a time, Njoroge was shaken all over. He thought he was going to be sick.

'Murdered?' he hoarsely whispered in utter unbelief. And all of a sudden a strong desire to know if Mwihaki was safe caught him. He for a moment forgot that he was addressing his enemies.

The white men closely watched him.

'Yes. Murdered.'

'By whom?'

'You'll tell us that.'

'Me, Sir? But—'

'Yes. You'll tell us.'

Mr Howlands rose and came to Njoroge. He was terrible to look at. He said, 'I'll show you.' He held Njoroge's private parts with a pair of pincers and started to press tentatively.

'You'll be castrated like your father.'

Njoroge screamed.

'Tell us. Who really sent you to collect information in Jacobo's house about . . .?'

Njoroge could not hear: the pain was so bad. And yet the man was speaking. And whenever he asked a question, he pressed harder.

'You know your father says he murdered Jacobo.'

He still screamed. Mr Howlands watched him. Then he saw the boy raise his eyes and arms as if in supplication before he became limp and collapsed on the ground. Mr Howlands looked down on the boy and then at the officers and walked out. The red beard and the grey eyes laughed derisively.

Njoroge was not touched again and when he became well a few days later, he and his two mothers were released.

The hut in which he had been put was dark. Ngotho could not tell day or night. For him, darkness and light were the same thing and time was a succession of nothingness. He tried to sleep on his sides but only his buttocks were safe. So from day to day he remained in the same sitting posture. But then sleep would not come to relieve him. He wanted to forget his life. For behind him, he was only conscious of failure.

The awareness that he had failed his children had always shadowed him. Even before this calamity befell him, life for him had become meaningless, divorced as he had been from what he valued.

In spite of his pain, however, he never regretted the death of Jacobo. In fact immediately after Jacobo's death, Ngotho felt grateful. This was an act of divine justice. For a day or two he had walked upright only later to hear that his son Kamau was arrested in connection with the murder. For a day and a half, he had remained irresolute. But at night he knew what to do. The Gikuyus said, 'We shall not give the hyena twice.' Now since the white man had reversed the tribal law and cried, 'A tooth for a tooth', it was better for Ngotho to offer his old tooth that had failed to bite deep into anything. But Ngotho could never tell where he had found courage to walk into the D.O.'s office and admit that he had killed Jacobo. It was a confession that had shocked the whole village.

And Ngotho had now for days been tortured in all manner of ways, yet would tell nothing beyond the fact that he had killed Jacobo.

Mr Howlands had, as was the usual practice with government agents and white men, taken the law into his own hands. He was determined to elicit all the information from the man. So he had Ngotho beaten from day to day. For Mr Howlands was determined to conquer and reduce Ngotho to submission.

Ngotho, who had worked for him and had thwarted his will,

would not now escape from him. For Ngotho had become for him a symbol of evil that now stood in his path.

And indeed he became mad where Ngotho was concerned. Even the homeguards who worked with him feared to be present when the D.O. was eliciting information from this man.

But Ngotho had stuck to his story.

Njoroge had always been a dreamer, a visionary who consoled himself faced by the difficulties of the moment by a look at a better day to come. Before he started school, he had once been lent to his distant uncle to help him in looking after cattle. The cattle had troubled him much. But instead of crying like other children, he had sat on a tree and wished he had been at school. For that would end such troubles. And for an hour he had seen himself grown up and at school. Meanwhile the cattle had eaten a good portion of a *shamba* and his uncle had to send him home immediately.

But all these experiences now came to Njoroge as shocks that showed him a different world from that he had believed himself living in. For these troubles seemed to have no end, to have no cure. At first these had a numbing effect so that he did not seem to feel. All he knew was that his father and his now only brother were in trouble and he himself was not at school.

But even when his mind became clear the old fear came back and haunted him. His family was about to break and he was powerless to arrest the fall. So he did not want to contemplate the fact that his father could have committed the murder. He did not even talk with Nyokabi or Njeri about it. And they perhaps understood him because they never tried to force it on him. Only one evening when every fire had gone out and voices in the village had died, did his mother try to speak to him.

'Njoroge.' The voice did not sound like hers.

'Yes, mother.' He feared her next word as he slightly held his breath. But she could not proceed. Njoroge could hear constant sniffs as if Nyokabi was unsuccessfully trying to suppress sobbing. He let his breath go. He felt a painful relief.

However, he could not all the time hold himself from thinking. The image of the murdered Chief as he had seen him in his home came to his mind. Everybody and everything for him had a stamped image of the chief. And this image came to represent that which had robbed him of victory when the door to success had been opened.

Only once did he think of Mwihaki. That was the night his mother had tried to tell him something. But he thought of her with guilt. He felt as if it was his connection with her that had somehow brought all this ill-luck. He wanted to shout to his mother across the night, *It's I who have brought all this on to you.* He hated himself without knowing why and then hated the Chief all the more.

Later this feeling became so oppressive that one night he left home. It was a quiet night and everyone had gone to sleep. Njoroge was long after to wonder how this courage had come to him. He walked towards the old house of the Chief, clenching his fists as if ready to fight. The ghost of the Chief was there to lead the way. And he followed it because he wanted to put an end to this oppression. He would revenge himself on the Chief and strike a blow for his family. But when he reached near the deserted household, the ghost had transformed itself into Mwihaki. He tried to hit her but soon realized that what he wanted was to hold her and together escape from the calamity around. She was his last hope. And then Njoroge woke up from what he thought was a frightening dream. He heard a sound of feet beyond the hedge that surrounded the house. He had forgotten that the deserted place was still guarded.

He quietly retraced his steps. In the morning he did not want to look his mother in the face because, even to him, the truth of his position was frightening.

That day for the first time, he wept with fear and guilt. And he did not pray.

CHAPTER SIXTEEN

Nyokabi and Njeri sat in a corner. Njoroge could see tears flowing down their cheeks. It depressed him because as a child he had been told that if women wept when a man was ill it showed that the patient had no hope. But even as Njoroge looked at the distorted face of his father, he had no strength to stop or soothe the weeping women. For the first time Njoroge was face to face with a problem to which 'tomorrow' was no answer. It was this realization that made him feel weak and see the emergency in a new light.

Ngotho struggled to one side and for the first time opened his eyes. Nyokabi and Njeri quickly moved nearer the bed. Ngotho's eyes roamed around the hut. They rested on each of the women in turn, Njeri first. He opened his mouth as if to speak. Instead a round tear rolled down his face. He wanted to rub it away. But as he could not lift his hand, he let the tear run down unchecked. Two others followed and Ngotho turned his eyes and rested them on Njoroge. He seemed to struggle with his memory. He then made an effort to speak.

'You are here. . . .'

'Yes, father.'

This rekindled hope in Njoroge. He felt a cold security when he saw that his father was still in command.

This was Ngotho's first speech since they moved him from the homeguard post, four days before. Njoroge was long to remember the day. Ngotho had to be supported by a man at either side. His face had been deformed by small wounds and scars. His nose was cleft into two and his legs could only be dragged. For four days now his mouth and eyes had remained shut.

'You come from school—'

'Yes, father.'

'To see me—'

'Yes.' He lied.

'Did they beat you there?'

'No, father.'

'Then – you – come to laugh at me. To laugh at your own father. I'll go home, don't worry.'

'Don't say that, father. We owe you everything. O, father, what could we do without you?' Njoroge bit his lower lip.

Ngotho went on, 'Your brothers are all away?'

'They'll come back, father.'

'Ha! At my death. To bury me. Where's Kamau?'

Njoroge hesitated. Ngotho continued, 'Perhaps they'll kill him. Didn't they take him to the homeguard post? But why do— They don't want an old man's blood. Now, don't ask, Did I kill Jacobo? Did I shoot him? I don't know. A man doesn't know when he kills. I judged him a long time ago and executed him. Ha! Let him come again. Let him dare. . . . Oh, yes, I know – Oh! They – want – the – young – blood. Look there, there – ah, they have taken Mwangi – Was he not young?'

Ngotho rambled on. All the time his eyes were fixed on Njoroge.

'I am glad you are acquiring learning. Get all of it. They dare not touch you. Yet I wish all my sons were here . . . I meant, ha, ha, ha! to do something. Ha! What happened? Who's knocking at the door? I know. It's Mr Howlands. He wants to get at my heart. . . .'

Ngotho's laughter was cold. It left something tight and tense in the air. By now darkness had crept into the hut. Nyokabi lit the lantern as if to fight it away. Grotesque shadows mocked her as they flitted on the walls. What was a man's life if he could be reduced to this? And Njoroge thought: Could this be the father he had secretly adored and feared? Njoroge's mind reeled. The world had turned upside down. Ngotho was speaking. Except for his laughter, his words were surprisingly clear.

123

'Boro went away. He found me out – a useless father. But I always knew that they would change him. He didn't know me when he came. . . . You see . . .'

Njoroge turned his head. He was aware of another presence in the room. Boro was standing at the door. Njoroge had seen him enter. His hair was long and unkempt. Njoroge instinctively shrank from him. Boro went nearer, falteringly, as if he would turn away from the light. The women remained rooted to their place. They saw Boro kneel by the bed where Ngotho lay. And at once, long before Boro began to speak, the thruth came to Njoroge. He could only hold his breath.

Ngotho could not at first recognize Boro. He seemed to hesitate. Then his eyes seemed to come alive again.

'Forgive me, father – I didn't know – oh, I thought—' Boro turned his head.

The words came out flatly, falteringly. 'It's nothing. Ha, ha, ha! You too have come back – to laugh at me? Would you laugh at your father? No. Ha! I meant only good for you all. I didn't want you to go away—'

'I had to fight."

'Oh, there – Now – Don't you ever go away again.'

'I can't stay. I can't.' Boro cried in a hollow voice. A change came over Ngotho. For a time he looked like the man he had been, firm, commanding – the centre of his household.

'You must.'

'No, father. Just forgive me.'

Ngotho exerted himself and sat up in bed. He lifted his hand with an effort and put it on Boro's head. Boro looked like a child.

'All right. Fight well. Turn your eyes to Murungu and Ruriri. Peace to you all – Ha! What? Njoroge look . . . look – to – your – moth —'

His eyes were still aglow as he sank back into the bed. For a moment there was silence in the hut. Then Boro stood up and whispered, 'I should have come earlier. . . .'

124

He ran quickly out, away from the light into the night. It was only when they turned their eyes to Ngotho that they knew that he too would never return. Nobody cried.

CHAPTER SEVENTEEN

The one road that ran across the land passed near the Indian shops. A few human voices mingled with an occasional hooting of a passing lorry or a car. The women came to the shops, saw him and suddenly stopped conversation.

'I want that dress.'

'And that bright one.'

'Aren't you selling?'

They talked at once, shouting across the counter as if they were talking to someone who was far away, someone who would never come back. One woman whispered to her neighbour, 'Don't be hard on the boy! You know what he has gone through. . . .' But her companion shouted all the more.

'Don't you hear?'

Njoroge roused himself. His voice was weary. His eyes were dull. He dragged his feet to a corner and brought the dress the women wanted. He did not want to look at them in the face because he thought they would see the dreams of his boyhood and laugh at him. The Indian sat in his own corner munching some green beans or ground-nuts. Njoroge was disgusted with the munching sound . . . *O, I wish he could stop.*

'How much?'

'Three a yard.'

'I'll give you two.'

He hated being driven on like this. He had lost the will to fight even in a bargain, and he was tired of this game. Life too seemed like a big lie where people bargained with forces that one could not see.

'There is no other price.'

'Don't lie!' the same woman shouted with real indignation. 'Why do you treat us as if you were an Indian?'

Njoroge flinched under this attack. As he watched them go out, he groaned inside. He had been made to work for the Indian by sheer necessity. The Indian left his corner and called the women back. He quickly sold them another dress of the same quality for four shillings a yard. Njoroge did not stir.

As the women finally left, two of them stopped a little and turned their eyes as if to sympathize with him. Njoroge wanted to hide. For he knew that they – the ones he had thought he would come to save – would go on discussing him and his family.

Five months and people still talked about it. It was as if the death of Mr Howlands on the same night that Ngotho had died was of a greater consequence than all the deaths of those who had gone before. But this case was more striking because all of one family was involved. Boro and Kamau were facing murder charges.

It had all happened on the day that Ngotho died. Mr Howlands had been in his sitting-room, all alone. Occasionally he looked at the ceiling and then tapped the table. A bottle of beer stood empty at a corner with a half-full glass in front. Mr Howlands had defiantly returned and stuck to his home in the dying farm. He could never get away from it. For the farm was the woman whom he had wooed and conquered. He had to keep an eye on her lest she should be possessed by someone else.

That night he was angry. He did not know what had happened to him since he saw something in the eyes of Ngotho's son. He had remembered himself as a boy, that day so long ago when he had sat outside his parents' home and dreamt of a world that needed him, only to be brought face to face with the harsh reality of life in the First World War. ... Mr Howlands could now remember only drinking to make himself forget. He cursed horribly.

And this Ngotho. He had let him go home more dead than alive. But still he had let him go. Howlands had not got the satisfaction he had hoped for. The only thing left to him was hatred. What had made him release Ngotho was a notebook that had been found behind the lavatory from where apparently Jacobo had been shot. The notebook had Boro's name. At first Mr Howlands had been unable to understand. But gradually he realized that Ngotho had been telling a lie, in order to shield Boro. But Boro was in the forest? Slowly he arrived at the truth. Ngotho too had thought that it was Kamau who had done the murder. He had taken on the guilt to save a son. At this Mr Howlands' hatred of Ngotho had been so great that he had trembled the whole night. He had drunk, itching to get at Ngotho but in the morning realized that he could not do what he had contemplated.

He looked at the door. He was expecting some policemen and homeguards with whom he went on night patrols. At last he stood up and began to walk across the room. He did not know why he now missed his wife. He wondered if he would go and get the black woman he had taken the night before. He had discovered that black women could be a good relief.

The nightly patrols had always been a special pleasure for Mr Howlands. They gave him a feeling of power and strengtl..

The door opened. Mr Howlands had not bolted the door. He glanced at his watch and then turned round. A pistol was aimed at his head.

'You move – you are dead.'

Mr Howlands looked like a caged animal.

'Put up your hands.'

He obeyed. Where was his habitual guardedness? He had let a moment of reflection unarm him.

'I killed Jacobo.'

'I know.'

'He betrayed black people. Together, you killed many sons of the land. You raped our women. And finally you killed my father. Have you anything to say in your defence?'

Boro's voice was flat. No colour of hatred, anger or triumph. No sympathy.

128

'Nothing.'

'Nothing. Now you say nothing. But when you took our ancestral lands—'

'This is my land.' Mr Howlands said this as a man would say, This is my woman.

'*Your* land! Then, you white dog, you'll die on your land.'

Mr Howlands thought him mad. Fear overwhelmed him and he tried to cling to life with all his might. But before he could reach Boro, the gun went off. Boro had learnt to be a good marksman during the Second World War. The white man's trunk stood defiant for a few seconds. Then it fell down.

Boro rushed out. He felt nothing – no triumph. He had done his duty. Outside, he fired desperately at the police homeguards who barred his way. But at last he gave up. Now for the first time he felt exultant.

'He's dead,' he told them.

Children came to the shop. They were coming from school. Njoroge saw their hopeful faces. He too had once been like this when he had seen the world as a place where a man with learning would rise to power and glory. Then he would never have thought that he would even work for an Indian. And suddenly Njoroge saw himself as an old man – an old man of twenty.

The children were frightened by his blank stare. They scampered away before he could arouse himself to do anything. The Indian left his corner.

'You are fired,' he shouted.

Njoroge had worked for less than a month. Money was badly needed at home.

'All right,' he said as he wearily walked to the road wondering how he would break the news to Njeri and Nyokabi. And he all at once wished that he had been a child and Mwihaki was near him so he could pour out all his troubles to her. And he knew that he had to see her.

CHAPTER EIGHTEEN

Saturday. Mwihaki sat outside her new home in the homeguard post. Her face had a strained look. She stood up and went behind the house. She took out the small note and read again. The strong appeal was there all right. But now that she had accepted to meet him she felt hesitant and guilty. She wondered what it was that he so much wanted to tell her. She had promised herself that she would not meet Njoroge again, when she had learnt about the painful murder of her father. For she felt betrayed by Njoroge. If what her mother had told her was true she would never have anything to do with the boy.

She had learnt about her father's death while at school. The headmistress had broken the news to her. For a short time she had been unable to believe that what the teacher was telling her could have anything to do with her father. Even when she had known without any doubt that he was dead she had been unable to cry. At night she thought about it. But she did not feel anything. No pain. It was only when she was on her way home that the full meaning of what had occurred broke upon her like a revelation. The horror of the calamity that had befallen Kenya came home to her in a new light. She had wept as she had never done before.

And now that she had agreed to go and meet a member of the family that had deprived her of a father, she was surprised at herself. But she wanted to meet him because at the very height of the crisis in her family the words that had most comforted were those that Njoroge had spoken to her. She had repeated them to her mother, saying firmly, 'The sun will rise tomorrow'. So, far from losing faith in God, she had put all her

trust in Him hoping that in heaven she would maybe meet her
father again.

Njoroge came to the place. He was glad that she had agreed
to meet him. For the fear that she might ignore him was the one
thing that had made him keep away from her all those months.
He did not know what he would tell her, for the knowledge that
Jacobo had been killed by his brother weighed heavily on him.
But she now meant to him more than anything else. It was late
in the afternoon when he reached the spot. Mwihaki was there
before him, a little farther down than the place where they had
met before. He saw that she had grown thinner. Her former
softness seemed to have hardened so that she appeared to have
all of a sudden grown into a woman. Mwihaki looked at Njoroge.
She saw frustration and despair and bewilderment in his eyes.
But she was determined to have no pity. So she just eyed him.

Njoroge looked down for a moment. Then at the plain
below. The silence between them was embarrassing. He did not
know how to begin or even what to say.

'I have come,' were her first words.

'Can't we sit down?'

'You can tell me what you want to say while we are standing.' When, however, he went and sat down she followed him
but sat far from him. He took a piece of dry stick and broke it.
She watched him stonily and then all of a sudden a tear ran
down her face. She quickly rubbed it. He did not see.

'Mwihaki, it is strange that you and I should meet under
these circumstances.' He now raised his eyes and faced her
boldly. 'I have known you for all those years when I was young
and foolish and thought of what I could do for my family, my
village, and the country. I have now lost all – my education, my
faith and my family. It's only now that I do realize how much
you had meant to me and how you took an interest in my
progress. Because of this it makes it all the more painful what
my people have done to you. I, alone, am left. Hence the guilt
is mine. I wanted to meet you and say that I am sorry.'

131

'Don't lie to me, Njoroge, surely you could have dropped me at least a warning—'

'I say I am guilty. But God – he – I knew no more about your father's death than you did.'

'Do you want to tell me that you – No!' She knew full well that it had been she who had asked him to go with her to her home. She kept quiet, He looked away.

'Mwihaki, I don't want to pretend that I would have warned you if I had known about it. But I assure you that I am deeply sorry. Please accept what I am telling you, for I love you.' At last he had said it. For now he knew that she was his last hope. He did not turn round to face her even when she had stayed for quite a time without saying anything.

'Njoroge!'

He moved his head slightly. Her eyes had softened. He almost broke down.

'Mwihaki, you are the one dear thing left to me. I feel bound to you and I know that I can fully depend on you. I have no hope left but for you, for now I know that my tomorrow was an illusion.' He still spoke in an even voice. Her eyes had a distant look in them. Njoroge thought she was ignoring him and looked away again. It was only when she had called him again and he saw tears in her eyes that he felt encouraged.

'I am sorry for having thought ill of you,' she said.

'No, Mwihaki. I must take on the guilt and you have all the cause to hate me,' he said, moving nearer to her. He held her left hand in his. She did not resist him and neither did she resist the tears that now flowed freely down her face. She tried to speak but something choked her throat. She struggled within herself. She must not lose control. Yet it seemed hopeless because she wanted him to go on holding her by the hand and lead the way.

'Don't! Don't!' She at last struggled to say. She knew that she had to stop him before he went very far. Yet she felt unequal to the effort and she blamed herself for having come.

132

And Njoroge went on whispering to her appealing to her with all his might.

'Mwihaki, dear, I love you. Save me if you want. Without you I am lost.'

She wanted to sink in his arms and feel a man's strength around her weak body. She wanted to travel the road back to her childhood and grow up with him again. But she was no longer a child.

'Yes, we can go away from here as you had suggested when—'

'No! no!' she cried, in an agony of despair, interrupting him. 'You must save *me*, please Njoroge. I love you.'

She covered her face with both hands and wept freely, her breast heaving.

Njoroge felt sweet pleasure and excitedly smoothed her dark hair.

'Yes, we go to Uganda and live—'

'No, no.' She struggled again.

'But why?' he asked, not understanding what she meant.

'Don't you see that what you suggest is too easy a way out? We are no longer children,' she said between her sobs.

'That's why we must go away. Kenya is no place for us. Is it not childish to remain in a hole when you can take yourself out?'

'But we can't. We can't!' she cried hopelessly.

Again he was puzzled. As a child Mwihaki had seemed to be the more daring. She saw the hesitancy in him. She pressed harder.

'We better wait. You told me that the sun will rise tomorrow. I think you were right.'

He looked at her tears and wanted to wipe them. She sat there, a lone tree defying the darkness, trying to instil new life into him. But he did not want to live. Not this kind of life. He felt betrayed.

'All that was a dream. We can only live today.'

133

'Yes. But we have a duty. Our duty to other people is our biggest responsibility as grown men and women.'

'Duty! Duty!' he cried bitterly.

'Yes, I have a duty, for instance, to my mother. Please, dear Njoroge, we cannot leave her at this time when – No! Njoroge. Let's wait for a new day.'

She had conquered. She knew now that she would not submit. But it was hard for her and as she left him she went on weeping, tearing and wringing her heart. The sun was sinking down. Njoroge's last hope had vanished. For the first time he knew that he was in the world all alone without a soul on whom he could lean. The earth went round and round. He saw everything in a mist. Then all of a sudden, he fell on to the ground and cried 'Mwihaki, oh Mwihaki.'

Sunday. Njoroge left his two mothers and wandered alone. Nyokabi watched him go out. She did not want to ask him where he was going. And she and Njeri did not speak about his going because they feared. . . .

Njoroge's trousers fluttered in the wind. The path was familiar and yet long and strange. He dragged his feet along. He met women, some going home from their various places before darkness came. Njoroge avoided their contact. He avoided their looks because he did not want their never-ending sympathy and pity. They would only see despair in his eyes. He kept on saying, 'I would have done it! I would have done it!' But he had wanted to see the two women and sleep under the same roof for the last time. He recalled Ngotho, dead. Boro would soon be executed while Kamau would be in prison for life. Njoroge did not know what would happen to Kori in detention. He might be killed like those who had been beaten to death at Hola Camp. O, God – But why did he call on God? God meant little to him now. For Njoroge had now lost faith in all the things he had earlier believed in, like wealth, power, education, religion. Even love, his last hope, had fled from him.

The land stretched on, unfolding its weird plainness to the eye. There were many who were now beyond the call of the land, the sun and the moon – Nganga, the barber, Kiarie, and many others. . . . The path eventually led him to the big and broad road. He followed it.

The voice was still urging him: *Go on!* He quickened his steps as if this would hurry the vanishing hours of day. It was night that was now welcome to him. The voice became more *Go on!*

But he said, 'Wait for the night'. He came to the bend of the road and instinctively looked up. It was there, there, that she had left him after declaring her love. The plain was on his right. He moved from the road that had no beginning and no end and went to the slope that extended from the road to the plain. He sat on a rock. He took out of his pocket the carefully folded cord. He felt a certain pleasure in holding it. For the first time he laughed alone. And he sat there waiting for darkness to come and cover him.

He knew the tree well. He had been there a number of times for the voice had often spoken to him many times after his father's death. The only thing that had restrained him was the hope that he might find an anchor in Mwihaki . . . He had prepared the rope.

'Njoroge!'

He stopped. He laughed to himself hysterically. The rope hung from a tree and was still in his hands. He heard again the voice, full of anxiety.

'Njoroge!'

This time the voice was clear. And he trembled when he recognized its owner. His mother was looking for him. For a time he stood irresolute. Then courage failed him.

He went towards her, still trembling. And now he again seemed to fear meeting her. He saw the light she was carrying and falteringly went towards it. It was a glowing piece of wood which she carried to light the way.

'Mother.' He felt a strange relief.

'Njoroge.'

'I am here.'

Nyokabi clung to him. She did not ask anything.

'Let's go home,' she commanded weakly.

He followed her, saying nothing. He was only conscious that he had failed her and the last word of his father, when he had told him to look after the women. He had failed the voice of Mwihaki that had asked him to wait for a new day. They met Njeri who too had followed Nyokabi in search of a son in spite of the curfew laws. Again Njoroge did not speak to Njeri but felt only guilt, the guilt of a man who had avoided his responsibility for which he had prepared himself since childhood.

But as they came near home and what had happened to him came to mind, the voice again came and spoke accusing him: *You are a coward. You have always been a coward. Why didn't you do it?*

And loudly he said, 'Why didn't I do it?'

The voice said: *Because you are a coward.*

'Yes,' he whispered to himself. 'I am a coward.'

And he ran home and opened the door for his two mothers.

Northcote Hall
July 1962

The African and Caribbean Writers Series

The book you have been reading is part of Heinemann's long established series of African and Caribbean fiction. Details of some of the other titles available are given below, but for further information write to: Heinemann International, Halley Court, Jordan Hill, Oxford OX2 8EJ

NGŨGĨ WA THIONG'O
Devil on the Cross

Written secretly in prison, on lavatory paper, while the author was detained without trial, the novel is a powerful critique of modern Kenya.

A Grain of Wheat

'With Mr Ngũgĩ, history is living tissue. He writes with poise from deep reserves, and the book adds cubits to his already considerable stature.'

The Guardian

Petals of Blood

A compelling novel about the tragedy of corrupting power, set in post-independence Kenya.

'. . . Ngũgĩ writes with passion about every form, shape and colour which power can take.'

Sunday Times

STEVE BIKO
I Write What I Like

'An impressive tribute to the depth and range of his thought, covering such diverse issues as the basic philosophy of black consciousness, Bantustans, African culture, the institutional church, and Western involvement in apartheid.'

The Catholic Herald

NELSON MANDELA
No Easy Walk to Freedom

A collection of the articles, speeches, letters and trials of the most important figure in the South African liberation struggle.

OLIVER TAMBO
Oliver Tambo Speaks –
Preparing for Power

This selection of speeches, interviews and letters offers a unique insight into the ANC President's views on the history of the freedom struggle within South Africa and, of even greater importance, his vision for the future.